DEATH, TEXAS STYLE

Blade burst from the alley to find a battle being waged.

Geronimo, Lieutenant Garber, Private Griffonetti, and Private McGonical were under assault from dozens of assailants. Grungy figures lined the roofs, were framed in windows, or had taken cover behind every available shelter.

Blade saw a tall man on the roof across the street let fly with an arrow from a compound bow. The shaft sped true, slicing into Griffonetti's throat and protruding out the back of his neck. Without a moment's hesitation, Blade angled the M-60 upward and squeezed the trigger. The heavy slug tore into the assailant and catapulated him from sight.

A man and a woman were charging from the right, each with a chain looped around their waist, each armed with a sword.

Blade pivoted, lowering the machine gun's barrel, and sent several rounds into each foe. They were flung to the road on their backs, kicking and shaking in their death throes.

A chunk of brick struck Blade on the right temple, filling his head with excruciating pain, and he twisted and glanced up to discover a man with a beard in a second-floor window, about to hurl a bigger piece of brick. Blade gritted his teeth and fired, and the man screeched as he staggered backwards and vanished. . . .

Also in the *Endworld* series by David Robbins:

ENDWORLD

#20: DALLAS RUN

DAVID ROBBINS

LEISURE BOOKS   NEW YORK CITY

Dedicated to Shane —
this one is for you, Little Guy.

A LEISURE BOOK®

March 1990

Published by

Dorchester Publishing Co., Inc.
276 Fifth Avenue
New York, NY 10001

CHAPTER ONE

Nelson hated border-guard duty.

He squinted up at the bright April sun, mentally cursing the Civilized Zone Army. While he was at it, he also cursed his immediate superior officer, Lieutenant Garber, and the commander of the armed forces, General Reese. For good measure he added in President Toland, the heat wave, and life in general.

Six more months, he told himself.

Six more months and he could kiss the damn Army goodbye! His two-year enlistment would be up and he could return to civilian life. He'd be free again! Free to let his hair grow if he wanted, free to wear whatever clothing he liked, free to stay out as late as he desired or to sleep in until noon without having an officer or a noncom standing over his bunk and bellowing for him to get his lazy butt out of the sack.

Oh, sweet freedom!

Nelson smiled at the thought of his honorable discharge, and shifted his attention to the stark, oddly ominous structures silhouetted against the southern horizon. The skyscrapers of Dallas, even at a distance of 15 miles, gave him the willies. He recalled all the horror stories he'd heard about the savagery reigning in the former metropolis, about the scavengers and the gangs and the mutations, and he wondered why anyone in their right mind would choose to live there, to exist in such squalor and filth amidst such danger. Living in Dallas didn't make any sense, not when the Civilized Zone border was so close.

He gripped the strap of the M-16 slung over his left shoulder with his left hand and rested his right on the top rail of the gate blocking off Highway 289. Sweat beaded his brow under his helmet and caked his sides under his green fatigue shirt. He longed for a cool drink or a cold bath. In four hours, at six P.M., he would be off duty, and he could hardly wait to strip off his uncomfortable uniform and sink into a tub of icy water.

"Daydreaming about Cindy, Art?"

Nelson started at the sound of the familiar voice and pivoted to his left to find Sergeant Whitney emerging from the white hut at the side of the road. "No," he blurted out.

"What's with you?" Sergeant Whitney asked, and grinned. "Why are you so jumpy?"

Nelson shrugged. "Didn't realize I was, Bob."

"I could understand a case of nerves if we were pulling the night shift," Whitney mentioned, stretching and staring at the far-off skyscrapers. "But it's the middle of the afternoon, for crying out loud."

"I guess pulling sentry duty at this post gives me the creeps," Nelson said.

"Me too," Sergeant Whitney admitted. "Those screams an hour ago were some of the loudest I've heard. It sounded like some poor woman was being torn limb from limb."

Nelson remembered and shuddered. Screams and wails from the direction of the decrepit, crumbling city were not uncommon, but during the past week all of the men pulling shifts at Sentry Post 17 had noticed an increase in the number of such cries, as if an unidentified terror stalked the inhabitants and was slaying them one by one. "Potts told me that on his shift last night he heard someone screeching for nearly an hour."

"You can't believe Potts. You know how that turkey likes

to exaggerate," Sergeant Whitney said.

"Yeah," Nelson agreed, glad he was on duty with a reliable, disciplined man like Bob Whitney. The two had known one another for seven months, ever since Nelson had been assigned to the Southern Perimeter Command, the unit responsible for manning all of the sentry posts along the southern border of the Civilized Zone. Despite their difference in rank and career status, with Whitney planning to stay in the Army for 20 years and hoping to eventually become an officer, they had developed a mutually respectful friendship. Nelson had taken his sweetheart, Cindy Hampton, over to the Whitneys on several occasions.

"One of these days General Reese will get his wish and be allowed to take a battalion into Dallas to clean out the scavengers and the other grungy riffraff," Sergeant Whitney remarked.

"I'm surprised he hasn't already," Nelson responded.

"General Reese can't make a move into the Outlands without President Toland's permission, and Toland is a politician."

"So?"

Whitney made a snorting noise. "You must not know much about politics. Politicians, Art, always take the path of least resistance. When faced with a crucial problem, they'd rather cower in a corner than take the bold stand necessary to solve the problem."

"I still don't understand," Nelson said.

"Permit me to educate you," Sergeant Whitney said, and pointed toward the city. "Out there lies the Outlands. Any and all territory lying outside of the boundaries of the organized factions is considered part of the Outlands."

"Tell me something I don't know."

"Okay, smart-ass. There are those who advocate assembling a huge force composed of a regiment from the Civilized Zone and elements from each of the other six factions in the Freedom Federation. They want this super detachment to venture into the Outlands and eliminate the raiders, the mutants, the gangs, and anyone or anything else that stands in the way of progress.''

"Sounds like a great idea to me," Nelson commented.

"There are many people who don't agree," Whitney noted. "They believe our armed forces are overextended as it is, what with maintaining the peace and protecting our borders. Any large-scale excursion into the Outlands might leave us open to attack from one of our enemies. There's also the issue of governmental control. Some people don't think the Civilized Zone, or any other Federation faction, has the right to annex additional land without the consent of the inhabitants of the Outlands. These people even have a motto." He paused. " 'Government by the people, not over the people.' "

"So you're saying that President Toland won't authorize a military strike into Dallas or any other part of the Outlands because a lot of voters would be upset with him?" Nelson queried.

"Give the man a gold star," Sergeant Whitney quipped.

Nelson pondered the implications for a moment. "But who knows what's going on out there? For all we know, there could be someone in the Outlands organizing an army to invade us."

"Could happen," Whitney acknowledged.

"What will it take to bring President Toland to his senses?" Nelson wondered.

"A brain transplant."

They both started laughing, but the laughter died abruptly seconds later when a high-pitched shriek rent the sluggish air, arising from a cluster of dilapidated buildings less than 200 yards from the sentry post, on the right side of Highway 289.

"What the hell!" Nelson exclaimed, unslinging his M-16.

Sergeant Whitney placed his right hand on the butt of the Browning semiautomatic strapped to his right hip. "Damn! I've never heard one that close before."

"Do we check it out?"

"You know better," Sergeant Whitney replied. "We stay put."

Nelson listened with bated breath, the short hairs at the nape of his neck tingling. Between the gate and the buildings stretched a field of brush and scrub trees in which nothing moved. On the left side of the roadway an expanse of field extended for over 500 yards before ending at a row of abandoned frame homes, many of which were partly collapsed. "I don't see anything."

"Keep your eyes peeled," Sergeant Whitney directed. "I'm going to call this in." He turned and entered the sentry hut.

A drop of sweat trickled onto Nelson's left eyelid, and he mopped at his brow with the back of his left hand, feeling annoyed at himself for his excessive nervousness. Why was he so antsy? He'd pulled guard duty more times than he could count, and he'd never felt so apprehensive before. Was his mind playing tricks on him, or was it trying to warn him of impending peril? He took a few deep breaths to steady himself.

Another shriek sounded, louder than the previous cry.

Nelson glanced at the hut and saw Sergeant Whitney using the radio to contact Lieutenant Garber. He licked his lips and scanned the field on the right, and a flicker of movement approximately a hundred yards from the gate drew his attention. His brown eyes narrowed and he leaned forward.

The bushes in a thicket were shaking violently.

He raised the M-16 to his shoulder and sighted on the center of the thicket, hoping the cause of the movement was just a mutation of some kind, a two-headed coyote or a six-legged skunk or some other form of genetically warped animal. In the 106 years since World War Three, mutations had proliferated. Encountering genetic deviations was an ordinary occurrence. The ecological chain had been severely disrupted by the massive amounts of radiation and chemical-warfare toxins unleashed during the holocaust, and physical deformities were commonplace in all wildlife. According to an article he'd read in the *Army News,* the experts believed that embryonic development was no longer predictable. So if a four-eyed rabbit or a feral dog with two tails should pop out of that thicket, he wouldn't be surprised.

The bushes ceased shaking.

Nelson breathed a sigh of relief and relaxed, lowering the

M-16 to his waist. How could he allow himself to become so worked up over a lousy moving bush? He grinned at his stupidity, and the grin froze on his face when a figure, doubled over at the waist and racing too fast for details to register, darted from the thicket into a patch of tall weeds. Shocked disbelief rooted him to the spot for all of three seconds, and then Nelson dashed toward the hut. "Sarge! Sarge!"

Whitney appeared in the doorway, an M-16 in his right hand. "Calm down, Art. What is it?"

"I saw someone," Nelson reported, and pointed at the thicket.

"Only one?" Sergeant Whitney asked, walking to the gate and peering at the field.

"Yeah."

"Male or female?"

"I couldn't tell."

"Were they armed?"

"I couldn't tell," Nelson said, embarrassed by his lack of perception. "I caught a glimpse of someone running into the weeds, but I couldn't distinguish any features."

They waited in an expectant silence for over a minute, but nothing else happened.

"I know I saw someone," Nelson insisted.

"And I believe you," Whitney assured him.

"What did the lieutenant say?"

"I didn't speak to him," Sergeant Whitney answered. "Dutch told me that Lieutenant Garber is at Sentry Post 19. There was an incident there two hours ago."

"What kind of incident?"

"Dutch wouldn't tell me. But he's relaying our message to the lieutenant."

Nelson pursed his lips, troubled by the news. Dutch Miller was the Communications man on duty at headquarters, and Dutch would never withhold information unless under direct orders, which meant the top brass had clamped a lid on whatever had transpired at Sentry Post 19.

"Listen," Sergeant Whitney said. "Do you hear that?"

"What?" Nelson responded, tilting his head. "I don't—" he began, and then he heard the sound too, a peculiar low intonation coming from far to the south. "What is it?"

"Chanting, I think. Dozens of people."

"Who the hell would be chanting out *there*?"

"Beats me," Sergeant Whitney said with a shrug. "But I don't like it one bit."

"Me neither," Nelson concurred. The chanting had a droning, rhythmic quality, rising and falling in an eerie cadence, the individual words, if there were any, indistinguishable.

"I'm calling for reinforcements," Sergeant Whitney announced, and went to take a step, but he glanced down the road and did a double take. "Do you see what I see?"

Nelson looked, and for a moment doubted his own vision. A white horse and rider were approaching the sentry post at a sedate pace. One instant the highway had been empty, and the next they were in the middle of the road, as if they had materialized out of thin air, near the structures about 200 yards away.

"Where'd they come from?" Nelson asked.

"Maybe they came from behind those buildings and we didn't notice," Sergeant Whitney conjectured.

Nelson squinted, discerning dark, flowing, shoulder-length hair on the rider. "It's a woman!"

"Yep."

"What's a woman doing out here in the middle of nowhere?"

"How should I know?"

"Where'd she get a white horse?" Nelson asked in astonishment.

"What I'd like to know," Whitney said, "is where are her clothes?"

Nelson studied the rider, his eyes widening in amazement as he realized Whitney spoke the truth. The woman appeared to be naked! Except for the hair falling over her breasts, she wasn't wearing a stitch of clothing. "This can't be happening.

I must be dreaming.''

"Cover her," Sergeant Whitney instructed, resting the barrel of his M-16 on the top rail.

"Do you want me to frisk her when she arrives?" Nelson asked hopefully.

"Wait until I tell Cindy on you," Whitney joked.

The woman rode ever closer, the clopping of the horse's hoofs growing louder and louder. Her right hand held the reins, her left lay on her left thigh.

"Who are you?" Sergeant Whitney called out when the woman was 50 yards off. "What do you want?"

She did not reply.

Sergeant Whitney wagged the M-16. "Didn't you hear me? What's your name?"

Still she came on without responding.

"Do you want me to shoot her?" Nelson offered in jest. "She might be hiding a hand grenade in her hair." He chuckled at his own joke and stared at the woman. At a range of 40 yards he could see a smile on her rather lovely features. He also saw strange greenish dots on her body, dots that grew in size with each passing yard until, at 75 feet, the dots had blossomed into distinct green splotches marking her skin from her chin to her feet.

Sergeant Whitney had also seen them. "Halt!" he shouted. "Stop where you are!"

But again the woman refused to acknowledge the noncom.

"I'm warning you!" Whitney yelled, elevating the M-16. "This is an official entry point into the Civilized Zone. No one enters without permission. Stop or I'll shoot."

The naked woman continued to ride toward them.

"Please! Halt!" Whitney commanded, and aimed at her forehead. "I'll count to three, and then I'll fire."

Nelson watched her move forward, flabbergasted by her audacity.

"One!" Sergeant Whitney declared.

She smiled even more broadly.

"Two!"

The woman was only 20 yards from the gate when she unexpectedly reined in. "Hello," she greeted them in a pleasant, melodious voice. "Don't shoot me."

Sergeant Whitney slowly lowered his M-16. "Who are you?"

"My name is Marta," the woman said. She leaned down to pat her mount on the neck, exposing her large breasts to their view. "This is Victor."

"I'm Sergeant Whitney of the Civilized Zone Army," the noncom informed her, and motioned at Nelson. "This is Private Nelson. I'm afraid we can't allow you to proceed any further north. We'll have to notify our superior officer of your presence. You can't enter the Civilized Zone unless Lieutenant Garber personally approves your admittance and you pass your physical." He paused and eyed her quizzically. "You *do* want to enter, don't you?"

"We plan to, yes," Marta said, straightening.

"Then I must make a call," Whitney said. "But first, would you mind telling me why you're not wearing any clothes?"

The woman laughed lightly and ran her left hand through her long hair. "It's too hot for clothes, don't you think?"

"It's hot," Sergeant Whitney agreed, "but most folks don't strip off all their clothing just because it gets hot."

"Neither do I."

Whitney's brown eyes narrowed. "But you said it's too hot to be wearing clothes, and you're naked."

Marta beamed at the noncom and winked. "Noticed, huh?" She giggled. "Men always notice."

"Why *did* you take off your clothing?" Sergeant Whitney asked.

"I didn't," Marta replied.

"But you're not wearing any."

"I never do."

Sergeant Whitney and Nelson exchanged puzzled expressions.

"Pardon me, miss, but I don't quite understand," Whitney remarked. "Do you mean you always go around nude?"

"Nudity is purity, and purity is the Mark."

"What mark?" Whitney asked.

"The Mark of the Chosen."

Nelson listened to the exchange in bewilderment. The woman's bizarre behavior inclined him to the opinion she was off her rocker. From the tales he'd heard, he knew the Outlands teemed with wackos, unfortunate crazies whose dementia could be attributed to their parents ingesting foodstuffs tainted by the radioactive and chemical poisons polluting the environment. He looked at Whitney and rolled his eyes.

"Well, Marta, I'll have to insist that you remain where you are while I contact the lieutenant," the noncom told her.

"Can I come a little closer?" Marta requested, and nudged the white horse with her ankles before Whitney could answer.

"That's close enough."

"I won't bite," Marta said, and grinned impishly, advancing nearer, to within 15 yards.

"Stop!" Sergeant Whitney barked.

She reined up. "Okay. Okay. Don't lay an egg. I can't believe hunks like you two are scared of little old me."

"We can't take any chances," Sergeant Whitney said. "There's a possibility you're infected with a disease."

"I am not," Marta responded indignantly.

"Then what are those green spots all over you?"

Marta touched one of the inch-wide irregular splotches on her left thigh. "Do you mean these?"

"What are they?"

She traced the outline of the splotch with her finger. "Isn't it beautiful?"

"Miss?"

"Such exquisite design. The Maker is magnificent."

Sergeant Whitney glanced at his companion. "She needs a psychiatrist," he whispered, then faced the woman and raised his voice. "When did you break out in those green spots?"

Marta looked up in surprise. "These? I've had these all of my life."

"You were born with them?" Sergeant Whitney inquired.

"Yes. Some of the Chosen are born with the Mark, some are converted."

"I'm sure they are," Whitney said. "Watch her," he ordered Nelson, and walked into the sentry hut.

"What's your name again?" Marta asked the private.

"Nelson. Art Nelson."

"Were you born with the Mark?"

"I wasn't born with green spots on my body," Nelson responded.

"None whatsoever?"

"None," Nelson verified.

"How sad," Marta declared and frowned. "But then we can't be blamed, can we?"

"Blamed for what?" Nelson asked.

"For the outworking of the Maker's will."

"I don't follow you."

"We follow the Lawgiver, and the Lawgiver has decreed the cleansing of the Earth."

Nelson repressed an impulse to cackle. Her nonsensical talk indicated how severely unbalanced her mind must be. He felt a degree of sympathy for the woman and hoped the doctors would be able to assist her.

"Where are you from?" Marta asked him.

"I was born and rasied in Denver," Nelson disclosed.

"Where's Denver?"

"North of here about seven hundred and eighty miles."

"Do any of the Chosen dwell in Denver?"

"Who are the Chosen?" Nelson rejoined.

"You have ears, but you don't hear," Marta said, and sighed. "When the final roll call is made, where will you be?"

Nelson didn't know what to say, so he held his tongue.

"When the final roll call is made, I'll be counted on the side of righteousness and glory," Marta said.

"That's nice," Nelson replied politely.

"I have served the Lawgiver faithfully for all my years," Marta went on. "My name will be entered on the scroll of glory.''

''I hope it's spelled correctly,'' Nelson quipped, looking at the hut. He saw Whitney seated at a table. The noncom's back was to the sole window, and on the table next to his left arm sat the radio. A headset perched on the sergeant's head. His shoulders were slumped, as if he was dejected over something.

''I hope you'll forgive us for our deception,'' Marta said.

''Deception?'' Nelson repeated absently, still gazing at Sergeant Whitney, mystified because his friend wasn't moving. Her words abruptly sank in, and he looked up at the woman, befuddled by her comments. ''Us? Who are you talking about?''

''Why, my brothers and sisters, of course,'' Marta said, smiling sweetly and motioning at the field on the right side of Highway 289.

Dread engulfing him, Nelson pivoted toward the field, his confounded expression transforming into a petrified one at the sight of the grim, unnatural swarm closing on Sentry Post 17. Goose bumps erupted all over his flesh, and he spun toward the hut. ''Sarge!'' he shouted, taking a stride, only to see two more appear in the doorway as Whitney toppled from the chair.

Marta laughed.

Private Art Nelson raised his M-16, squeezed the trigger, and screamed in abject terror.

CHAPTER TWO

"Do you see them, pard?"

"Nope."

"What about you, you mangy Injun?"

"No sign of them. And if you call me that again, I'll scalp you."

The three men were lying flat on their stomachs on the east side of a low hill, less than a yard below the rim. Trees and undergrowth surrounded them except on the crown of the hill.

"I reckon I'll take a gander," proposed the man lying on the right, a lean figure attired in buckskins and moccasins. Around his slim waist were strapped a matched pair of Colt Python revolvers. Blond hair and a blond moustache accented his handsome features. His alert blue eyes narrowed as he edged cautiously higher.

"Do you think it's safe?" asked the stocky Indian on the left. He wore a green shirt and green pants, both sewn together from the remnants of an old canvas. In contrast to his blond associate, his hair was black, his eyes brown. Secure in a shoulder holster under his right arm rested an Arminius .357 Magnum, while tucked under his deer-hide belt above his right hip was a genuine tomahawk.

"If it's a trap, we'll soon know," said the man in the middle, a seven-foot giant wearing a black leather vest, green fatigue pants, and black combat boots. On each hip rode a Bowie knife snug in its sheath. A comma of dark hair hung above his gray eyes. His most outstanding attribute was his awesome physique; he bulged with layer upon layer of rippling muscles. Even while lying prone on the ground he emanated an aura of raw power.

"How far are we from the base?" the gunman in the buckskins asked, pausing below the crest.

"I estimate about two hundred yards," answered the Indian.

The gunman inched to the top and lifted his head for a glimpse of the slope on the opposite side. "All I see are trees and more trees," he whispered.

"Figures," the Indian muttered.

"What's that crack supposed to mean?" the gunman demanded, sliding from the rim.

"It means you couldn't spot them if they were sitting on the tip of your nose, Hickok."

"Is that so?" Hickok retorted.

"White men need binoculars to see anything more than ten yards away," claimed the Indian.

"And I suppose Injuns don't?"

"Every Indian is endowed with the exceptional vision of an eagle. We can spot a fly at five hundred yards, a bear a mile off. Why do you think your race always used members of my race as scouts and guides back in the ancient times of the Old West?" the man in green responded.

"Because the whites needed somebody who knew which leaves were safe to use," Hickok cracked.

"Excuse me for interrupting," the giant said, "but there *is* the little matter of getting safely through enemy territory to the base." His voice became stern. "The next one who opens his big mouth will pull extra wall duty for a month. Is that clear, Hickok?"

"Yeah, pard," the gunman replied, then grumbled. "What a grump!"

"Is that clear, Geronimo?" the giant addressed the Indian.

"Clear as a bell, Blade."

"Good. Now let's reach the base without being detected,"
Blade proposed. He rose to his knees, scanned the west slope
of the hill, and nodded. "The coast is clear. Let's go." He
stood and jogged over the crest, winding between the trees
and skirting any boulders in his path.

Hickok and Geronimo dutifully followed.

Blade came to the edge of a clearing and halted, taking his
bearings by the position of the morning sun, calculating he
had 150 yards to go. He was about to step into the clearing
when he observed a small form scurry into concealment behind
a pine tree less than 20 yards to the south. A grin creased his
lips.

"There's one on our trail," Geronimo suddenly whispered.

Blade glanced over his right shoulder. "Did you see him?"

"No, but I know he's there."

The loud snap of a dry twig sounded to their rear, confirming
Geronimo's assertion.

"Okay," Blade said quietly. "They know where we're at.
Stealth is no longer important. Let's make a dash for the base."

"It'll be a piece of cake," Hickok said. "Those turkeys can't
catch us."

"I'm ready," Geronimo said.

"Then let's do it," Blade said, and took off, racing westward, vaulting all obstacles, heedless of the noise he created.
A recently tilled field appeared 30 yards ahead, and he bore
to the left, intending to go around it rather than disturb the
rows of meticulously planted seeds. He was almost to the
southwest corner when he realized he'd done exactly as the
opposition had expected.

Between the corner of the field and the forest rose an
enormous bur oak, 70 feet in height with a stout trunk four
feet in diameter. A path ran along the edge of the tilled field,
passing within two feet of the tree.

Blade angled onto the well-used path. He came abreast of
the bur oak and glimpsed a diminutive shape leaping at him
from the cover of the tree trunk. He tried to twist aside, to
evade the hand clawing at his vest. Thin fingers snatched at

the leather and a squeal of triumph attended the contact.

"I got him!" a childish voice cried.

Hickok and Geronimo fared no better.

The gunman, laughing heartily at Blade's capture, tried to turn and escape. Instead, he inadvertently collided with Geronimo, and before either could hope to flee another pygmy-sized opponent came around the other side of the tree trunk and slapped both of them on their butts.

"We did it!" the elated winner shouted. "We won!"

Hickok placed his hands on his hips and glared at Geronimo. "Smart move, you cow chip! This is the third time we've lost."

"Why didn't you tell me you were going to reverse direction?" Geronimo countered. "Do you think I can read your feeble mind?"

"You couldn't read a first-grade primer without help."

Blade smiled down at the two boys congratulating one another for a job well done. A third boy burst from the brush and joined their group.

"Did we win again?" the third boy asked.

"They didn't stand a chance!" stated the boy who had tagged the giant. He stood four feet in height and possessed a remarkable physical build for his size and age. His eyes were blue, his hair black. A short-sleeved brown shirt and faded blue pants covered his powerful frame. He looked up at Blade. "Did you let us win, Dad?"

"No, Gabe," Blade answered. "You won honestly."

"I got my dad and Geronimo!" boasted the second child, who in every respect was a carbon copy of his father; the same blond hair, the same lean figure, even the same style of clothing in the buckskins and moccasins he wore.

"Don't get a swelled head over it," Hickok admonished the youngster. "You wouldn't have caught me, Ringo, if Geronimo wasn't such a klutz."

"My daddy isn't a klutz!" said the third boy, whose Indian lineage was readily apparent. Like his father, he had on a green shirt and pants.

"Thanks for sticking up for me, Cochise," Geronimo said, placing his right hand on his son's left shoulder.

"Wait until Mommy hears we won again!" Ringo said.

"There's no need to tell her," Hickok said testily.

"Why not?" Ringo asked.

"Yeah, why not?" Blade added, baiting the gunfighter.

"Well, you know how women are," Hickok responded.

Blade grinned and crossed his arms on his chest. "No. Tell us."

"Yeah, tell us," Geronimo said.

"What are women like, Daddy?" Ringo asked innocently.

"Women are contrary critters," Hickok said seriously. "They have a hard time understandin' things that are important to a man, like huntin' and fishin' and guns and such."

"But Mommy likes to hunt and fish, and she has her own M.A.C. 10 and two revolvers," Ringo pointed out.

"Yeah, but she's a Warrior like me," Hickok said, defending his line of reasoning. "She's not like most women, which is one of the reasons we got hitched."

"I still want to tell Mommy we beat you three times," Ringo persisted with the single-minded determination of a young boy who was only eight months shy of his fifth birthday.

"Your mom and your sister have been busy cleanin' our cabin all morning," Hickok said. "If we tell Sherry that we've been playin' War Tag, she'll accuse me of goofing off while she's workin'."

"You *have* been goofing off," Geronimo said dryly.

"Who asked you?" Hickok retorted.

Blade chuckled and ambled to the west. "All of us should be getting back. Lunch will be in half an hour." He looked down as his son came up on his left.

"Why does Uncle Hickok always say things that get him in trouble with Aunt Sherry?" Gabriel asked earnestly.

"I can answer that," Geronimo interjected. "Hickok suffers from the dreaded foot-in-mouth disease."

"Do you, Daddy?" Ringo asked his father.

"Don't listen to Geronimo," Hickok advised. "He thinks

he's a regular comedian.''

"What's a comedian?" Ringo asked.

"Someone who says and does funny things all the time," Hickok explained.

"Like you?" Ringo responded.

Blade and Geronimo cackled.

The three men and their sons strolled toward a row of cabins visible 60 yards ahead. Birds chirped in nearby trees. Squirrels scampered on a maple tree they passed. Two white butterflies flitted above the tilled field.

Gabe took hold of his father's brawny hand. "It sure is nice having you at the Home. I missed you when you were away all the time."

The corners of Blade's mouth curled downward, and he sighed and stared at the azure sky. He felt the same way. The past five and a half months had been the happiest he'd experienced in years. Being able to spend precious days with his wife and son had rejuvenated him, had improved his disposition 100 percent. He wasn't susceptible to as many bouts of temperamental moodiness. Life held meaning again. The seemingly endless cycle of taking on one enemy after another, of battling each and every threat to the Family and the Federation, had been broken. Except for the fight against the Union the previous month, he'd savored five and a half months of relative peace and tranquility. And he didn't want the idyllic interlude to end.

Was it only January of last year that he became the head of the Freedom Force? he asked himself. So much had happened since then—so many close friends had lost their lives. Friends who had relied upon him, upon his judgment and ability. What sort of insanity had induced him to try and hold down two posts entailing supremely critical responsibilities simultaneously? He must be an idiot. Unbidden memories flooded his mind.

He owed his first post to the wealthy survivalist who had founded the 30-acre compound in northwestern Minnesota prior to World War Three. Kurt Carpenter had expended

millions of dollars to have the retreat constructed to his
specifications. A 20-foot-high brick wall afforded the first line
of defense against the bands of scavengers and raiders who
roamed the land, pillaging and slaying at will. Barbed wire
crowned the wall, and an inner moat flowing along the base
of all four sections served as yet another fortification as well
as supplying the water for Carpenter's descendants. The
Founder, as Carpenter became known, had dubbed his compound the Home and named his followers the Family.

In a world deranged by a cataclysm of unprecedented
proportions, the Home was an oasis of sanity. In a land where
civilization had regressed to the level of barbarism prevalent
in the Dark Ages, the Family exalted the highest ideals of
spiritual brotherhood. Encompassed as they were by hostile
elements, the Family would soon perish were it not for the
special, elite class of diligently trained men and women whose
primary duty was to safeguard the Home and protect the
Family, a class known far and wide as the Warriors. Time
and again the Warriors had eliminated threats to the Family's
welfare, and in the process the 18 members of the unique
fighting group had acquired a respected reputation as
formidable adversaries.

The Family had encountered other organized factions
devoted to preserving some semblance of prewar culture. Two
of the factions were also located in northern Minnesota: the
Clan to the west of the Home and the Moles to the east. In
the Dakota Territory dwelt the rugged horsemen known as the
Cavalry. In Montana the Flathead Indians ruled. A large
section of the Midwest was now called the Civilized Zone.
And on the West Coast the Free State of California was one
of the few states to retain its administrative integrity after the
war. Together these seven factions formed a mutual-defense
league designated the Freedom Federation. Naturally, when
the leaders of the Federation had decided to form a strike force
to deal with any and all menaces, they'd asked Blade to head
their brainchild, the Freedom Force.

Which posed a major problem.

Because Blade was already the head of the Warriors.

He chided himself for stupidly agreeing to perform both jobs when his intuition had warned him that he might be biting off more than he could chew. For almost a year he'd commuted between the Home and the Freedom Force facility situated near Los Angeles. For almost a year he'd been lucky to spend more than a week out of each month with his wife and son. For almost a year he'd pushed himself to the limit, ranging from Florida all the way to Alaska on missions against Family or Federation foes.

The toll on his personal life had been devastating. His wife had pleaded with him to devote more time to his family. Both Jenny and Gabe had felt neglected, and they had been profoundly upset by his prolonged absences. The strain on his emotional state had grown with each assignment. Finally, after battling a maruading band of pirates in Canada, and after three members of the Force had died, he'd decided to disband the Freedom Force for a year so he could remain at the Home and give every spare moment to his wife and son. Unless an emergency arose, he didn't want to be bothered by the Federation leadership.

That had occurred six months ago. The Federation had managed to get by without calling on his services once, and he hoped six more months would elapse before they would call on him again.

Blade squeezed his son's hand and smiled. "You don't have to worry. I have no intention of leaving again for quite a while."

"Mommy has been happier with you home," Gabe mentioned.

"I know," Blade said, thinking of the many tender moments Jenny and he had shared during the past six months, more than in the four years before combined.

"Mommy says you may go to California again," Gabe said, his tone reflecting his anxiety at the prospect.

"Six months from now I may have to go," Blade said. "But we'll cross that bridge when we come to it."

"I hope you don't," Gabe said.

"You and me both," Blade said.

"I hope you stay too," Geronimo chimed in.

"Why's that?" Balde asked over his left shoulder.

"Because Hickok is in charge of the Warriors when you're away from the Home, and having him in charge is like playing Simon Says with a simpleton," Geronimo said.

"Says who?" the gunfighter demanded.

"Practically everybody."

Blade grinned. "Don't you worry either," he said to Geronimo. "I'm not going anywhere anytime soon."

Hickok started to speak, but before he could utter a syllable the very ground seemed to quake as, with a deafening, thundering roar, a gleaming silver jet streaked in low over the Home, flying at treetop level, swooping directly over the gunfighter and his friends.

"It's one of the Federation Hurricanes!" Ringo cried.

Blade watched the aircraft arc into the blue sky with a sinking sensation in his stomach.

CHAPTER THREE

She stood outside the cabin doorway, her green eyes on the Hurricane circling above the Home, absently brushing at her blonde bangs with her right hand, worry etched in her features. In her left hand she clutched the white towel she had been using to wipe the dishes. A yellow blouse and blue pants hugged her shapely form.

"Mommy! A Hurricane!" came a yell from her right.

Struggling to compose herself, she turned, facing her husband and son, forcing a smile. "It certainly is," she said enthusiastically.

"Can we go up for a ride?"

"Not today, Gabe," she told him.

"Awwww, Mom. Why not?" Gabe asked, hurrying the last ten yards to the cabin.

"Someone must be here on official business," she explained. "They probably won't have the time to take us up."

"We could ask," Gabe suggested.

"You heard your mother," Blade said, halting three feet away and gazing at the craft.

"But Dad—" Gabe began.

"Don't argue," Blade said. He stared into his wife's eyes, reading the anguish they conveyed, and glanced over his right shoulder. Hickok, Ringo, Geronimo, and Cochise were angling to the south, heading for their respective cabins.

"Hey, Jenny!" Geronimo called, and waved.

"Hi," Jenny said, acknowledging the greeting, her eyes locked on her husband.

"Go inside and wash your hands for lunch," Blade instructed his son.

"I want to go see the jet land," Gabe said.

"You can see the jet after you eat," Blade said.

"It might fly off by then," Gabe said.

"The Hurricane will still be here. Go wash your hands," Blade ordered.

"Gee, I never get to have any fun," Gabe mumbled. He dutifully turned and entered the cabin.

"Any idea why the Hurricane is paying us a visit?" Jenny inquired the moment the boy was inside.

"None," Blade answered.

"No clue at all? It certainly isn't the usual courier flight."

Blade discerned the skepticism in her tone, and knew she suspected him of withholding information. "If I knew, I'd tell you."

"It's not here to pick you up?" Jenny asked.

"I don't know why the jet is here," Blade insisted. "I'd better go find out." He took a step.

Jenny moved in front of him, preventing him from advancing. "What if they want you to accept another assignment?"

"We don't know if they do."

"Why else would a Hurricane arrive at the Home unexpectedly? A crisis must be brewing somewhere and they need you to ride to the rescue like you always do," Jenny said bitterly.

Blade placed his hands on her shoulders and spoke tenderly. "What if they do need me? Would you have me refuse?"

"You could."

He frowned and stared at the ground. "You know I can't."

"Why not?" Jenny demanded. "Why must you always be the one? Why can't one of the other Warriors go instead? You don't need to lead every mission."

Blade looked at her, his brow knitting. "I can't run from my responsibilities. I'm the head Warrior and I'm the head of the Force. When they need me, I must go."

Frustration formed in the lines of her lovely face and she clenched her fists. "It's not fair, Blade! It's just not fair! We're finally back to normal as a family again. Gabe will be broken-hearted if you leave."

"We don't know if I have to," he reiterated, and took her into his arms. For several seconds she angrily resisted his embrace, and he could feel the tenseness in her shoulders and arms. Gradually Jenny relaxed, her left cheek pressing against his chest, her right arm draped around his broad back.

"I'm sorry," she apologized huskily.

"I understand."

"It isn't fair for me to take out my resentment on you," Jenny said.

"Believe me, I understand," Blade reiterated, as always sensitive to her innermost thoughts and emotions. They had been sweethearts since childhood, and over the years an intuitive bond had developed between them, an almost clairvoyant perception of each other's sentiments and desires. His sensitivity made him all the more distressed whenever his duties required him to leave the Home on extended runs. To him, being separated from Jenny and Gabe qualified as the ultimate torture. "Say—" he began, and coughed.

"Yes?"

"How would you react if I quit the Warriors?"

Jenny pushed back and glanced up. "What?"

"It's been six months since I flew off in one of the Hurricanes on a mission, and you're as upset now as you were back then. If my leaving is that much of an ordeal, if my position as the top Warrior and the head of the Force is having such a terrible effect on Gabe and you, then maybe I should seriously consider retiring from both," Blade proposed, and kissed her on the forehead. "Your happiness is more important to me than anything else in the world. I won't allow anything or anyone to ruin our marriage, to put a rift between us. I'd rather sacrifice my job than lose you."

Tears suddenly welled in her eyes, and she threw her arms about him and squeezed him tightly. "Oh, dearest!" she said. "I never meant for you to give up being a Warrior!"

Blade stroked her hair, waiting.

"Plato and the Elders believe you're the best Warrior the Family has ever seen, and I know in my heart they're right," Jenny went on. "Being a Warrior fits you to a T. You're perfect for the job, and you could no more stop serving the Family as a Warrior than you could stop breathing." She paused and took a breath. "The problem isn't your being the top Warrior. The problem is the Freedom Force post."

"I know," Blade said softly.

"Then just disband the Freedom Force permanently."

"The decision isn't mine to make," Blade replied, gazing at the Hurricane. "The leaders of the Federation formed the Force, and any final decision rests with them. I doubt they'd agree to disband the Force on a permanent basis. We have too many enemies who would gleefully grind the Federation into the dust. There's the Russians, the Technics, the Superiors, the Lords of Kismet, and others. We can't afford to be caught off guard. Freedom, as Plato would say, is only preserved through diligence."

"Then ask the Federation leaders to pick someone else to head the Force," Jenny suggested. "Hickok, Geronimo, Rikki, Spartacus, or Yama could handle the job, no problem."

"Any one of them could," Blade agreed.

"Will you ask?"

"In due time. I have six months in which to make up my mind about whether I'll stay on the Force or not. Until then, if an emergency should arise, I'll have to go."

"Why do I have the feeling that you're stalling?" Jenny asked.

"I might be," Blade conceded. "Sometimes the best way to solve a problem is to let it resolve itself."

"And sometimes the problem just becomes worse," Jenny

noted.

"True," Blade said, and stared at the jet again. The aircraft was descending slowly. As a VTOL, a jet with vertical-takeoff-and-landing capability, the Hurricane did not need a lengthy runway to land or take off. Much like a helicopter, the VTOL could drop to the ground or rise straight up. Once airborne, the unique aircraft could attain supersonic speeds on sustained flights. The Free State of California possessed a pair of Hurricanes, perhaps the only such aircraft in existence.

"You'd better go," Jenny said, moving aside, nervously wringing the towel.

"Be seeing you," Blade said, and kissed her lightly on the lips. He hastened westward, hoping that there was a logical, mundane reason for the presence of the VTOL. The two aircraft were frequently utilized to shuttle the Federation leaders to periodic conclaves, but the next conclave wasn't scheduled to be held for another two months. The jets were also used to run a monthly courier service between the Federation factions, and the last regular courier flight had been ten days ago. So the purpose behind the VTOL's visit must be something out of the ordinary.

"Hey, pard! Wait for us!"

Blade halted and turned to find Hickok and Geronimo jogging toward him.

"We dropped off the young'uns at my cabin," the gunfighter stated as they came within a few feet and stopped. "My missus will feed their faces, then get Jenny and Geronimo's squeeze and they'll all come find us."

"My *squeeze*?" Geronimo said. "She has a name, you know. And I'd wish you'd make up your mind."

"About what?" Hickok asked.

"About your vocabulary. One minute you're using that ridiculous, phony Wild West talk you like so much, and the next you're using everyday slang."

"What's wrong with that?" the gunfighter asked.

"It bugs me. You sound even more idiotic than usual."

Hickok made a snorting noise. "Excuse me for living. It's

not my fault you can't recognize eloquence when you hear it."

"Eloquence? Shakespeare was eloquent. Lord Byron was eloquent. Joseph Conrad was eloquent. Compared to them, you're mentally defective," Geronimo said, and paused. "Actually, compared to a *toad* you're mentally defective."

"I can palaver as good as the next bozo," Hickok said.

Geronimo looked at Blade. "I rest my case."

"Let's go," Blade directed, and headed for the west wall, knowing the VTOL would land in the cleared field outside the drawbridge. While the Founder had wisely foreseen many of the Family's needs and constructed and stocked the compound accordingly, Carpenter had not anticipated they would require a landing area for visiting aircraft. The eastern portion of the Home was preserved in its natural state or devoted to agriculture. In the middle of the 30-acre plot, in a line from north to south, were the cabins for the married couples and their children. The western section contained the enormous, reinforced concrete blocks devoted to specific functions. Arranged in a triangular fashion and designated according to letters, with A Block at the southern tip of the triangle, the blocks were positioned precisely 100 yards apart.

A Block housed the Family armory, with one of the greatest collections of weapons ever assembled. The sleeping quarters for the single Family members were in B block. C Block was the infirmary, where the Healers ministered to anyone who was sick or injured. A workshop area for the making of everything from furniture to shoes filled D Block. E Block contained a library that would have rivaled any in existence before the war, and F Block was devoted to gardening and farming and managed by the Tillers.

Access to the compound was over a drawbridge situated in the center of the west wall. The orignal drawbridge had been destroyed during a siege by an enemy army, and the replacement opened outward instead of inward. A massive wooden bridge between the base of the drawbridge and the compound proper enabled those entering or leaving to cross the moat.

Thanks to an ingenious design, the Family would never

experience a water shortage. A rechanneled stream flowed into the Home in the northwest corner, via an aqueduct, and was diverted into two streams along the base of the brick walls, converging again at the southeast corner, where the water passed through another aqueduct and meandered to the south.

"I wonder why that flyin' contraption came here," Hickok said.

"We'll soon know," Blade said.

The gunfighter rubbed his palms together and grinned. "Maybe we'll finally see some action."

"You hope there's trouble?" Blade responded curtly.

"We haven't seen any action in months. I'm gettin' rusty doing nothing but walkin' the ramparts and baby-sittin' the tykes," Hickok said.

Geronimo snickered. "If I recall correctly, you were the one who claimed he was tired of all the killing. On our last run, to Cincinnati, you told us you were all set to hang up your guns and take up knitting as a hobby."

"I never said any such thing," Hickok countered. "You were the hombre all prepared to stop being a Warrior, and I figured I'd go along with you to cheer you up."

"White Man speak with forked tongue," Geronimo said.

"Blade, you were there," Hickok mentioned. "Tell this snake in the grass how it really was."

"Don't involve me in your petty squabbles."

Hickok and Geronimo looked at one another.

"Did he say squabbles?" the gunman asked.

"Did he say petty?" Geronimo responded.

"What's eatin' you, pard?" Hickok asked the giant.

"Nothing," Blade said testily.

"Then why are you suddenly so cranky?" Hickok asked.

"Who's cranky?" Blade retorted.

"Is your missus on your case again?" the gunfighter asked, pressing the issue.

"I don't want to talk about it," Blade said. He surveyed the landscape ahead. Dozens of Family members were moving across the large area between the concrete blocks, hustling toward the open drawbridge.

"We're your pards, remember? If you're upset, we want to lend a hand," Hickok offered.

"You can help me by dropping the subject."

"Consider it dropped," Hickok said.

They walked in silence for all of five seconds.

"But if you'd like me to talk to Jenny, I will," Hickok volunteered.

Blade glanced at the Family's preeminent pistoleer. "You do and I'll break every bone in your body."

"Does that mean no?"

Blade increased his pace.

"I think you should talk to her," Geronimo whispered to the gunman.

"You do?"

"Sure."

"But you heard the Big Guy."

"Yep. That's why I think you should talk to her. You'll be giving Blade a chance to practice his self-control," Geronimo remarked.

"And what happens if he blows his lid?" Hickok asked.

Geronimo shrugged. "You'll be wearing a body cast for a year or so. No big deal."

The gunman's eyes narrowed. "Oh. I get it. You want him to beat me to a pulp."

"Heaven forbid," Geronimo said with an air of supreme innocence. "Besides, he couldn't beat your whole body to a pulp."

"Because I'm lean and mean?"

"No, because if he hit your thick skull he'd break his hand," Geronimo answered, and chuckled at his own joke.

"You're a funny man," Hickok said. "You'd be funnier if you had a sense of humor, but you're still a load of laughs."

"I have to be, working with you every day," Geronimo countered. "Otherwise I'd lose my mind."

"What mind?"

They hurried to the bridge over the moat, mingling with

other Family members, and moments later were standing outside the compound at the edge of the crowd gathered to gawk at the aircraft and welcome the occupants of the Hurricane. The brush and trees had been cleared for 150 yards in every direction from the brick walls, enabling the Warriors on guard duty on the ramparts to spot any raiders or mutations that might be tempted to attack the Home. Invariably when a Hurricane arrived at the retreat, the pilot would set the craft down in the field to the west of the drawbridge. Although the VTOL could come down in the tract between the concrete blocks, the pilot ran the risk of a stray child blundering too near the aircraft and being injured.

Four men were conversing next to the Hurricane.

An elderly man in a brown shirt and pants was addressing the others. Gray hair and a long gray beard framed facial features reflecting an innate dignity and wisdom. His wiry hands were clasped behind his stooped back.

To the right of the aged speaker stood two men in uniform. The taller of the pair wore the blue uniform of a captain in the Free State of California Air Force, and in his left hand he gripped a flight helmet. The second man wore the typical green uniform of an officer in the Civilized Zone Army. Gold insignia adorned his shoulders. His rugged visage showed him a man accustomed to being obeyed.

In front of the elderly man, his sturdy form clad in a blue suit, his black hair clipped short, was a figure who'd unconsciously adopted an attitude of self-importance. His suit was immaculate, his black shoes polished.

"Excuse me," Blade said, and politely proceeded through the crowd toward the VTOL. When still 15 yards from the quartet, he saw the blue eyes of the man in blue swing in his direction and a smile lit the other's face.

"Blade! Am I glad to see you! We've got trouble!"

CHAPTER FOUR

Blade extended his right hand as he advanced. "Hello, President Toland," he greeted the leader of the Civilized Zone.

The man in the blue suit took the Warrior's hand and shook it vigorously. "It's nice to see you again, Blade. I only wish the circumstances were different. We need to find a place to talk in private."

"Glad to see you, Blade," chimed in the Civilized Zone officer, nodding at the giant.

"General Reese," Blade said, and smiled at the other officer, the captain in the California Air Force. "Captain Laslo. We weren't expecting you for about three more weeks."

The pilot nodded at the VTOL. "Have wings, will travel. That's my motto."

Blade twisted and gestured at his companions. "All of you know Hickok and Geronimo."

More greetings were exchanged, and then the elderly man cleared his throat.

"Gentlemen, we should adjourn to E Block. I'm sure we can find a quiet corner in the library in which to hold our discussion."

"Whatever you say, Plato," President Toland responded. "Lead the way."

Plato nodded and led off through the crowd toward the drawbridge, and the rest fell in to his rear, except for Blade. The giant strolled on Plato's right, and Plato became aware that the Warrior was studying him intently. "Do I have food crumbs in my beard?"

"No," Blade said, and chuckled. "Nadine told me yesterday that you haven't been feeling too well lately."

"That wife of mine is worse than a mother hen," Plato groused. "A simple touch of the flu has escalated into a case of the bubonic plague. I'm physically fit, thank you. The Healers administered an herbal remedy that was remarkably efficacious."

President Toland, who was following directly behind Plato, overheard their banter. "Can these Healers of yours cure many diseases?"

"They are extremely skilled at treating all manner of ailments," Plato answered in his soft voice. "They adhere to the naturopathic method of treating illness as opposed to the allopathic, the homeopathic, or any of the other methods commonly employed before World War Three."

"I'm not a doctor. What's the difference?" President Toland inquired.

"There are major differences between the various methods," Plato elaborated. "The Healers could explain them much better than I can, although there is an example that might be instructive. Prior to the war, the physicians in many countries treated disease by injecting vaccines consisting of dead bacteria or virus particles into the patient in the hopes of inducing the patient's body to produce antibodies to fight the disease. Naturopathy, by contrast, uses herbs and food and heat and exercise to promote healing."

"And this naturopathic business works?" President Toland inquired, his tone tinged with skepticism.

Plato glanced over his right shoulder and smiled. "We've survived for over a century."

They crossed over the moat and angled in the direction of E Block.

President Toland inhaled deeply, then sighed. "You know, Plato, I envy you."

"Why?"

"For one thing, you're not cooped up in an office all day. Look at this compound. Fresh air. Sunshine. Kids playing. Birds singing. The whole atmosphere of the Home is restful and pleasant," Toland said. "But I spend an average day in my office, and all I have to stare at are four walls. From six in the morning until midnight, six days a week, I'm usually behind my desk. I read reports and sign documents and meet with government officials and other visitors to the capital in Denver. Venturing outdoors is a luxury I can rarely indulge. In my capacity as Chief Executive I attend scores of functions each month, and even then I seldom have an opportunity to really relax."

"Relaxation is essential to a fuller enjoyment of life. Periods of work must be alternated with periods of play," Plato advised.

"I know that," President Toland replied. "But the degree of our responsibilities is vastly different. You're the leader of approximately one hundred people and you oversee a thirty-acre compound. I'm the leader of a few million people, and there are about six hundred and fifty thousand square miles in the Civilized Zone. If our situations were reversed, I doubt you'd find much time to smell the roses either."

"I'd make time."

"Easier said than done," President Toland said. "I'm just glad I don't have a wife and children. I'd never get to see them." He paused. "But I guess a person has to make sacrifices in the name of service and duty."

"Sacrifice is one thing, martyrdom is another," Plato said. "When you deny yourself a family, when you forsake knowing the joy of binding with a woman and rearing children, you deprive yourself of an essential human experience. Devotion to duty is commendable, but not at the expense of your spiritual welfare."

President Toland listened attentively, and he wasn't the only one. Blade stared at his mentor, engrossed.

"The Elders have conducted an extensive study of prewar society," Plato mentioned in his pedantic style. "We know, for instance, that America was in a state of decline during the decades before the war. The major cities were war zones where drug addiction was epidemic and the police and the military battled gangs of violent youths. Illiteracy was widespread. Instead of teaching ennobling ideals and moral values, the schools taught an insidious humanist doctrine that advocated self-gratification and selfishness. Degeneracy flourished. Euthanasia was encouraged. Teenagers and college students committed suicide at a staggering rate, and the elderly were subjected to a public propaganda campaign designed to entice them to terminate their own lives so they wouldn't be a burden on the social structure. Most of the politicians, instead of having the interests of the people at heart, were power-mongers who loved money more than they did the idea of serving their fellow man."

"Are you implying I'm a power-monger?" President Toland asked.

"Not at all," Plato said. "You sincerely want to improve the conditions under which the citizens of the Civilized Zone live, and you won't allow vested interests to manipulate the people against their will." He looked at Toland and smiled. "At least, I hope you won't."

"What does all of this have to do with my not getting married?" Toland inquired.

"Our study of the prewar culture revealed an alarming fact," Plato disclosed. "The populace back then, particularly those in the industrialized nations, had allowed themselves to be swept up in the materialistic mania perpetuated by the money barons. In America, as an example, in order for a typical family to pay their monthly bills it was necessary for both the father and mother to work, leaving their children to be reared by strangers at establishments called day-care centers. Without the loving, nurturing guidance of their parents, the children were left adrift in a morass of immorality where the young ones were preyed upon by deviates and drug czars."

"I repeat," President Toland interrupted. "What does all of this have to do with me?"

"Simply this. Nearly everyone in America was infected by the status delirium. The quest for success dominated their lives. The almighty dollar became their god. Their marriages suffered. Their children suffered. Ultimately, the humanist doctrine of self-gratification destroyed the bedrock of their civilization, the foundation of all culture, the institution of the family and the home. Without the home, any civilization is doomed," Plato said, staring ahead at E Block. "Those prewar Americans and you have a lot in common, President Toland. Like them, you're stuck in a rut of your own making. You work yourself to death, and for what? I'm not belittling your devotion to duty, but I strongly suggest you have misplaced your priorities. Will the Civilized Zone government collapse if you take several days off? I doubt it. Will you be happier thirty years from now looking back on the memories of your civil service, or would you be happier remembering thirty years of sharing your life with the woman you love? You're snared in a frantic rat race, and the only one who can free you is *you*."

They covered several yards before President Toland spoke. "I never really thought of it that way. Your reputation for wisdom and compassion is well founded."

Blade merely gazed absently at the grass, contemplating the pertinence of Plato's remarks to his own life. Toland wasn't the only one stuck in a rut. Six months ago he'd reached the same conclusion, and he was no closer to resolving the dilemma. Some problems, evidently, were universal and decidedly difficult to overcome. He glanced at Plato and smiled. Ever since his father, the previous Family Leader, had been killed by a mutation, Blade had looked up to Plato for seasoned counsel. The sage had become a substitute father, in a sense, and the two had developed a deep bond of affection and friendship.

They were within 20 yards of the gigantic concrete bunker containing the hundreds of thousands of volumes personally selected by the Founder. Kurt Carpenter had attempted to envision the hardships the Family would face, and to stock books instructing his followers and their descendants on how to deal with those hardships. One of the largest sections in the library consisted of hundreds of books pertaining to survival skills. There were also reference books on every conceivable subject, as well as volumes on military strategy, history, hunting and fishing, gardening, woodworking, metalsmithing, weaving and sewing, natural medicine, geography, religion and philosophy, and many, many more. The library functioned as the Family's prime source of tutelage and amusement.

Plato stopped and faced their visitors. "Would you care for refreshments? You must be hungry after your long flight. I can send for some food before we begin."

"No," President Toland said. "I'm not hungry, and our business here is extremely urgent."

"Then let's get to work," Plato suggested.

In single file they entered the library and moved to a table in the northwest corner virtually surrounded by six-foot-high wooden shelves crammed with books. Plato took a seat at the head of the table with Blade, Hickok, and Geronimo to his right. President Toland, General Reese, and Captain Laslo sat on the left. Those Family members seated nearby courteously shifted to tables farther away to give the Family Leader and the three Warriors more privacy.

Plato rested his chin in his right hand and locked his inquisitive scrutiny on the president of the Civilized Zone. "What can be so urgent that a special trip to the Home is necessary?"

"I don't know where to begin," Toland replied, frowning and exchanging a worried glance with General Reese.

"I've seldom seen you at a loss for words," Plato mentioned. "What is the nature of the emergency?"

President Toland looked at Plato, then each of the Warriors.

"I hope I'm wrong. The evidence isn't conclusive, but there's a possibility we have a plague on our hands."

For a full ten seconds no one spoke. Blade felt his mouth go dry and licked his lips. Now he understood why Toland had displayed such an interest in the Family Healers.

"Can you elaborate?" Plato requested.

"Certainly," President Toland said. "It all began three days ago when two of our sentry posts in northern Texas were attacked. Sentry Post 17 and Sentry Post 19 are both located within twenty miles of the city once known as Dallas. Sentry Post 17 is approximately fifteen miles north of Dallas on Interstate 35. As you know, we have a network of sentry posts all along our borders. Raiders and scavengers are a constant problem, and our armed forces do an excellent job of defending our boundaries."

"What transpired at the two posts near Dallas?" Plato queried.

Toland looked at General Reese. "If you don't mind, I'll have the general give you the same briefing he gave me."

"Be our guest," Plato said.

The Civilized Zone's Chief of Staff cleared his throat, his brown eyes betraying an uncharacteristic anxiety. "At ten minutes before noon on April twelfth, Lieutenant Garber, the officer in charge of the sector in which Sentry Post 17 and Sentry Post 19 are located, received a call on the radio from the sergeant at Post 19. The sergeant reported that a naked woman on a black horse was approaching his position—"

"A naked woman?" Hickok interjected, and laughed. "You're pullin' our legs, right?"

"I assure you I am serious," General Reese responded indignantly. "That was the last report we received from the sergeant. Lieutenant Garber tried to raise Post 19 after five minutes elapsed and there was no follow-up, per regulations. When the communications man couldn't reach Post 19, Garber went to investigate. You'll never guess what he found."

"The sergeant and the naked lady eloped?" Hickok quipped.

Plato glanced at the gunman. "Nathan, please. This is a

grave matter.''

"Sorry, old-timer.''

"Please continue," Plato urged the general.

"Lieutenant Garber found nothing," General Reese revealed. "No sergeant, nor the private who was supposed to also be on duty, and no naked woman.''

"What about the black horse?" Hickok asked.

"No horse either," General Reese said gruffly. "There was no indication of a struggle. It was as if they vanished off the face of the earth.''

"Most peculiar," Plato commented.

"It gets stranger," General Reese declared. "About two hours later, while Lieutenant Garber and a platoon were at Sentry Post 19 conducting their investigation, the communications man at headquarters received two odd calls from Sentry Post 17. The sergeant at that post, Sergeant Whitney, first called in to report loud screaming very close to the sentry hut. A few minutes later he radioed in again, this time to report that a naked woman riding a white horse had shown up at the checkpoint.''

Hickok snorted.

"Sergeant Whitney was cut off in midsentence," General Reese detailed grimly. "When the message was relayed to Lieutenant Garber, he went immediately to Sentry Post 17. There was no sign of Sergeant Whitney, the private assigned there with him, or the woman on the white horse.''

"Wow! This is serious! We've got a passel of females traipsin' all over the countryside in their birthday suits and turnin' folks invisible," Hickok remarked.

General Reese leaned forward. "What *is* your problem?"

"You'll have to excuse Hickok," Geronimo interjected. "He's been this way since birth.''

"He has?" the general responded.

"I have?" Hickok asked.

"Yep," Geronimo answered. "Hickok is the only Family member who was ever born with a vacuum between his ears.''

"Mangy Injun," the gunfighter muttered.

Preoccupied with his concern over Jenny's probable reaction should he need to travel to Texas, Blade had sat staring at the table, absorbed in his dilemma. Now he swiveled in his chair and looked at Hickok and Geronimo. "I want to thank the two of you," he said.

"For what, pard?" Hickok asked.

"We've been close friends since childhood, right?" Blade asked.

"You know we have," Geronimo answered suspiciously.

"And we've been working together in the same Warrior Triad for most of our adult lives, right?"

"Yeah. So?" Hickok said.

"So I want to thank you for all of the practical experience in child rearing you've given me," Blade said. "Working with you two clowns is the same as working with a pair of four year olds, and I think I'm a better father because of it."

"Didn't he bring this up once before?" Geronimo asked Hickok.

"Some folks have a one-track mind," the gunman said.

"If either one of you interrupt again, I'll have to inflict the worst possible punishment," Blade told them.

"Extra wall duty?" Hickok asked.

"You'll assign us to the detail that clears the outer fields," Geronimo guessed.

"Wrong. I'll tell your wives that you've been acting your mental ages again."

"That's not fair!" Hickok declared, horrified at the prospect. "My missus would never let me hear the end of it."

"You have a mean streak a mile wide," Geronimo said.

Blade's features abruptly hardened. "Not another word."

Neither the gunfighter nor Geronimo responded.

Blade glanced at General Reese. "You can continue now, and I guarantee that no one will interrupt."

"Thank you," the officer replied. "Now where was I? Oh, yes. Lieutenant Garber found a few bloodstains at Sentry Post 17, but Sergeant Whitney and the private, a man named Nelson, had disappeared like the two men at Sentry Post 19.

The woman on the white horse was also gone.''

Blade glanced at Hickok, who sat quietly with his hands folded in front of him on the table.

"Lieutenant Garber decided to notify his superiors, and he was driving back to Sherman, where the command center for that sector is located, when one of the troopers in his jeep pointed out someone up ahead on the road. They saw a soldier staggering along as if he was drunk, but when they reached him and stopped they discovered he was in a state of shock. It turned out to be Private Nelson. They transported him to Sherman and our medical specialists examined him.''

"What caused the shock?" Plato inquired.

"We found out, eventually. Nelson wouldn't respond to interrogation for over twenty-four hours. He sat there like a vegetable, and the doctors were about to throw in the towel when we had a lucky break. A nurse tried to feed Nelson a meal, and when he saw a bowl of salad on his tray he went berserk. Started screaming and ranting and raving. The doctors calmed him down, and he told us that Sergeant Whitney had been captured by a group of crazies. Apparently, the woman on the white horse was a ruse to distract Whitney and Nelson while others snuck up on them unnoticed.''

"How did Private Nelson escape?" Blade questioned when the officer paused.

"He ran for his life," General Reese divulged. "He emptied his M-16, then fled into the brush to the north. One of the crazies managed to strike him a glancing blow with a steel bar on the side of the head, and he dropped his M-16 and took off. Several of them chased him for about five hundred yards, then inexplicably gave up the chase and returned to the sentry hut. Nelson saw them carting Sergeant Whitney, who he had presumed was dead, away to the south. The woman on the white horse smiled and waved at him. And they took their wounded and dead with them.''

"A very thorough operation," Plato remarked.

"Both of their attacks on our sentry posts were meticulously planned," General Reese said. "They weren't a typical band of raiders or scavengers. We suspect they came from Dallas, but we don't know for sure.''

"How do the attacks tie in with the plague?'' Plato asked.

"I can answer that,'' President Toland said. "Private Nelson reported there were three unusual aspects of the attackers. First, he claimed the woman on the white horse exhibited psychotic tendencies. In his words, he thought she was off of her rocker. Second, their attackers wore very little clothing. Loincloths for the men, and that was about it. Third, their bodies were covered with mysterious green splotches.''

Plato straightened in his chair. "Green splotches?''

"That's how Private Nelson described them. Irregular green marks about an inch in size.''

"And every attacker bore these marks?'' Plato asked.

"Every one,'' President Toland said. "Our scientists and medical experts believe the green splotches signify a transmissible disease. A plague.''

"Did you come here to request the aid of our Healers?'' Plato asked.

"No,'' President Toland said, and stared at the three Warriors. "We want to send a team into Dallas to investigate.'' He paused meaningfully. "We want Blade to go.''

CHAPTER FIVE

"Why Blade?" Plato demanded. "Why not simply send in one of your own men?"

"We could send in a squad of our own," President Toland said. "In fact, Lieutenant Garber has volunteered to venture into Dallas. But we want someone with extensive combat experience to go in, someone with a proven track record, someone who's a professional, not an amateur. Garber is a competent soldier, but he doesn't possess a fraction of the expertise Blade does."

"Surely you must have other officers with extensive experience who would go," Plato observed.

"A few," President Toland replied. "But they don't hold the special position Blade does. The Freedom Force was created to deal with extraordinary threats to the safety of the Federation, and there's no doubt that the situation in Dallas qualifies. Blade is the head of the Force, and this falls under his jurisdiction." He gazed at the giant Warrior. "I know you requested time off to be with your loved ones, but this is an emergency. We must determine the nature of the illness responsible for the green splotches as quickly as possible. If a new plague is spreading among the residents of Texas, our medical specialists must devise an antidote before the disease can infect the Civilized Zone and the other Federation factions.''

"Has Private Nelson developed any of the splotches?'' Plato asked.

"Not yet,'' President Toland said. "He's been placed in quarantine and is under twenty-four-hour observation. So far he hasn't displayed any peculiar symptoms.''

"So far,'' Plato repeated. "But there's no guarantee Nelson hasn't already contracted the disease. And there's no guarantee Blade won't contract the green splotches if he goes to Dallas.''

"There are no guarantees whatsoever,'' President Toland agreed. "We need to learn more about the disease, which is why we want to send a team in. It's imperative that we capture one of the infected inhabitants and subject that person to intense testing and study.'' He looked at the head Warrior again. "How about it, Blade? You haven't said a word one way or the other, and the final decision is yours to make. Will you go into Dallas or not?''

Blade stared at Toland and Reese, then pursed his lips and drummed his fingers on the table. "This mission promises to be extremely hazardous for whoever accepts it.''

"I won't deny that,'' President Toland said.

"Fighting armed opponents is one thing, contending with a new disease quite another,'' Blade said. "You need someone who can get in fast and get right out again with a prisoner, someone who is adept at penetrating enemy territory.''

"You took the words right out of my mouth,'' Toland said.

"As much as I hate to admit it, you're right,'' Blade said. "This is a job for the Force.''

President Toland beamed. "I knew you'd agree with me.''

"But there's one little problem,'' Blade said. "The Force was temporarily disbanded six months ago and all the volunteers returned to their homes. Reorganizing them on such short notice would take more time than we can afford.''

"You could lead Lieutenant Garber and a squad of our men into Dallas,'' President Toland suggested. "With you in command, I know Garber would succeed.''

"I could,'' Blade said.

"If you don't mind," Plato interjected, raising his voice, addressing Toland, Reese, and Laslo, "I'd like to speak with Blade alone. If Hickok and Geronimo would be so kind, they can take you to my cabin. Nadine will fix refreshments."

"We don't want to impose," President Toland said.

"Nonsense," Plato responded. "Nadine will be delighted to have the company. Blade and I will be along in ten or fifteen minutes."

"As you wish," Toland said, and rose.

Hickok and Geronimo also stood, and the gunfighter looked at Blade. "Can we talk yet?"

"Of course," the giant replied.

"If you're aimin' to go to Texas, I reckon I'll tag along," Hickok offered.

"This is a job for the Force," Blade observed. "You're a Warrior."

"So are you, pard," Hickok said. "I might not be a member of the Force, but our Family is a member of the Federation. If the Federation is threatened, then I have an obligation to help out."

"We'll discuss it later," Blade said.

"Suit yourself," Hickok replied, and headed for the doorway.

Blade watched them depart. He stretched and focused his attention on the man he respected most in the world. "What do you want to talk about?"

"You."

"What about me?" Blade asked.

"You're behaving oddly."

"I don't know what you mean."

Plato studied the Warrior's features. "I think you do. It's not like you to be so reserved. And a minute ago you gave me the impression you were endeavoring to convince yourself that President Toland was correct, although there are legitimate arguments against his proposal. You simply reiterated the points he'd made."

"He was right."

"Was he?" Plato countered. "I wonder. Granted, you have more combat experience than most men, but Toland could use his own personnel to enter Dallas and capture one of those with the splotches. You're not essential to such an operation, despite what the two of you said."

Blade frowned and leaned back, crossing his arms over his chest. "I'm the head of the Freedom Force. It's my job to go."

"The Force has been disbanded."

"I told the Federation leaders I would be available in an emergency, and this certainly is an emergency."

Plato stroked his beard, his keen eyes narrowing. "Why do I have the feeling that you are resigned to go no matter how many objections I pose?"

"I've got to go, Plato," Blade insisted.

"Send Yama or Rikki in your stead. Either one of them can accomplish the mission."

"No."

"It has to be you, is that it?"

"Yes."

"Do you view yourself as indispensable? Will the world fall apart if you're not there to save the day?" Plato queried somberly.

"I don't have a swelled head, if that's what you're getting at," Blade responded.

Plato leaned toward the giant, concern etching his countenance. "Then *why*?"

The Warrior rose and began pacing back and forth behind his chair, his hands behind his back, his brow furrowed. "The last thing in the world I want to do right now is leave Jenny and Gabe to go on another mission, especially in my capacity as the head of the Freedom Force. Jenny resents the fact I joined the Force, and I know the news will break her heart." He paused. "But like it or not, I *am* the head of the Force. I accepted the position, and I gave my word to the Federation leaders to do the best job I can. If I say no now, I'll let them down. Worse I'll let myself down. When a man gives his word, he should keep it."

"Then you're going out of a sense of guilt?"

"Partly, I suppose. I'll feel guilty if I don't go, but I'll feel guilty if I do. If I don't, and if they send someone else and the mission fails, I'll blame myself. If I do, and Jenny becomes even more upset than she already is, I'll blame myself. I'm caught in a bind, in a no-win situation. I feel like I'm being torn in half," Blade admitted.

Plato did a double take, his eyes troubled. "I've never seen you this indecisive."

"It's like I'm running in circles and there's no end in sight."

"I see," Plato said, and stared at the table.

"Do you have any advice I can use?"

Plato looked up. "I'd advise you to take an extended vacation after this mission is over. Spend a month with your family and limit your contact with others."

"I've been trying that for the past six months."

"Yes, but you've stayed here at the Home and attended to your daily duties as a Warrior. I want you to get away from it all. Take Jenny and Gabe to one of the lakes. Go fishing. Forget all about your problems. Commune with the Spirit. Recharge your soul."

Blade considered for a moment. "Jenny would be delighted. We could kick back and relax without interruptions."

"Why don't you go break the news to her?" Plato suggested. "The prospect of taking a vacation might alleviate her anger over the mission to Dallas."

"You're on," Blade said with a smile, and hurried from the library.

Plato frowned and slowly stood. He walked from E Block with his head bowed so none of the other Family members could see the apprehension on his face. The sunlight made him squint, and he glanced up to behold Blade jogging to the east. There went the man he loved as the son he'd never had, the man he'd personally picked to become the top Warrior ten years ago. He'd taken such pride in Blade's growth, in seeing Blade develop from an impetuous, temper-prone youth into a stable, resolute man, into a superb Warrior. And while all the Warriors were adept at their craft, Blade was the best of the best. Someday, Plato knew, legends would be related about the mightiest Warrior of all time.

Provided Blade lived long enough to provide the basis for those legends.

Plato ambled eastward, making for his cabin. He could still fondly recall the very first time he had really noticed the boy who would eventually figure so prominently in his life. Blade had been five years old at the time. Before then, Blade had simply been one of the many children laughing and playing about the compound. But one fine morning Blade's father had introduced his son to Plato, and Plato remembered his astonishment at learning such a strapping boy was a mere five years of age. He had looked into the youth's intelligent, frank eyes and marveled. "So this is your pride and joy?" he had said to Blade's father. "And he's only five? Big for his age. I see he has his dad's dark hair and abnormal gray eyes. There is character here. He will be a tribute to both his parents."

And so their friendship had begun.

He recollected the anguish he had felt the day Blade's father was killed by a mutate. Blade had been 20 at the time, and had taken the loss hard. The Warrior's mother had died while giving birth to him, and the loss of his father had filled his soul with sorrow.

Plato skirted a pine tree in his path, ruminating.

Blade's father had been the Family leader, and his sudden demise had left a vacancy the Elders urgently needed to fill. Plato hadn't been too surprised when they selected him. He'd known that Blade's dad had favored him over all the other potential candidates. Once installed, Plato had returned the favor by nominating Blade to be the head Warrior. Family Leaders were permitted to choose whoever they preferred as their chief of Home security.

So many years had elapsed since then.

So much had happened.

Plato would always be in Blade's debt for rescuing Nadine from the savage Trolls. He'd given his beloved wife up for lost, and he still felt a thrill whenever he reminisced about the day he took her in his arms again after being separated from her for seven hellish years. Her return had seemed like a miracle, and he owed the greatest happiness of his life to the brooding giant he'd taken under his wing.

How ironic life could be.

And how cruel.

He remembered the epic struggle the Family had waged against the infamous, wicked Doktor and Samuel the Second, the men responsible for the death of Blade's father. Only after the Family emerged victorious had Blade appeared to come to terms with the loss of his dad. Since then the Warrior had discharged his responsibilities superbly.

Until now.

Plato scowled, striving to suppress the anxiety he felt over Blade's curious behavior. He perceived that the Warrior was severely distraught, more so than Blade had let on, perhaps more so than the Warrior himself realized. Something was eating at Blade deep down inside, and for Blade to travel to Dallas in such a distracted frame of mind would not bode well for the mission.

What could be the matter?

Certainly Jenny's resentment was a contributing factor, and the hardships posed by holding the two jobs also influenced the Warrior's attitude, but Plato believed there was more to the change in Blade's disposition.

Worry gnawed at his mind.

The Warriors were trained to be decisive, to make snap judgments in the heat of combat, to remain calm and collected even when their lives were on the line. A moment's indecision could prove fatal. And in Blade's current condition, the Warrior was vulnerable.

If anything happened to—

"Hey, old-timer!"

Startled, Plato looked up, surprised to discover his cabin less than 40 feet away. Hickok and Geronimo were walking toward him.

"Where's Blade?" the gunfighter asked.

"He went to talk to Jenny," Plato answered.

"Darn. We wanted to bend the big galoot's ear," Hickok said, halting. "He's takin' us to Dallas whether he likes the notion or not."

Plato looked over the gunman's left shoulder at the cabin. "Where are our guests?"

"With your missus," Hickok replied. "She's feedin' them venison sandwiches and cookies. They'll gain ten pounds before she's done."

"Did Blade change his mind about going to Texas?" Geronimo inquired.

"No," Plato responded.

"Then let's go find the dummy and persuade him to take us," Hickok said to Geronimo.

"Nathan—" Plato began.

Hickok held up his right hand. "Oh, no you don't!"

"What?"

"You're not gettin' away with it this time," the gunfighter declared.

"What do you mean?" Plato asked, perplexed.

Hickok snorted. "Don't play innocent with me, old-timer. You're not talkin' me out of it."

"But—"

"Don't waste your breath," Hickok said, cutting Plato off. "You've pulled this stunt too many times in the past and I'm drawin' the line right here and now."

"What are you talking about?"

"I suppose you don't recollect the time Geronimo was missin' and I wanted to go after him? I suppose you don't recall talkin' me out of going?"

"Yes, I remember that," Plato said. "We had no idea where he was, and I requested that you wait a week in the hope he would return. Which he did."

"That's not my point. Who was it who tried to talk me out of going after Shane when he went off to fight the Trolls?"

"I did," Plato admitted. "But you went anyway."

"Don't nitpick," Hickok said.

"But I—"

"I'm not finished yet," the gunman said. "Who was it who stopped me from stompin' that Troll we captured into the dirt? You. I could go on and on, but you get my drift. You're always talkin' me out of this or that, but not now."

"I wouldn't think of it," Plato said, and smiled.

"You can talk until you're blue in the face," Hickok said, "and it won't do you a bit of good. Blade, Geronimo, and I are a unit. We're Alpha Triad, and you know danged well we've worked together for years. Where Blade goes, we go."

"As well you should."

"So go ahead and waste your breath," Hickok said. "See if it . . ." He abruptly stopped, his forehead creasing. "What did you say?"

"I agree with you wholeheartedly," Plato informed him. "If the two of you want to go on the run with Blade, then by all means you should."

"Is this a trick?"

Plato chuckled. "No. I believe the two of you should go with Blade. In fact, I will insist upon it."

Hickok glanced at Geronimo. "Did I miss something here, pard?"

"The only thing you're missing is a brain," Geronimo replied, then looked at the Family Leader. "Why will you insist?"

"I have a favor to ask of you," Plato said.

"You name it, you've got it," Hickok declared.

"If I can convince Blade to take you, I want the two of you to stay close to him on this run. Watch over him. Cover his back."

"We always cover his back," Hickok remarked. "We wouldn't let anything happen to him. His missus would kill us."

Plato placed his right hand on the gunfighter's left shoulder. "Nathan, I'm serious. Please watch Blade closely."

Surprised by the Leader's sincerity, Hickok blinked a few

times, then smiled. "Sure, old-timer. We'll baby-sit the big lug for you. It'll be a piece of cake."

"Thank you," Plato said, and headed for his cabin. "Now if you'll excuse me, I must tend to our visitors."

Hickok scratched his head and watched Plato walk off. "Now what the blazes was that all about?"

"I don't know," Geronimo responded, gazing thoughtfully at the Family Leader's back.

"I swear that man is becoming goofier the older he gets."

Geronimo glanced at his friend and grinned. "So what's *your* excuse?"

CHAPTER SIX

"So that's Dallas, huh? How many folks lived there before the war, pard?"

"About two million," Blade replied.

"I wonder how many are there now," Geronimo commented.

The three Warriors stood on Highway 289, next to the open gate at Sentry Post 17. Behind them, parked in a row from south to north on the right side of the road, were the 14 vehicles comprising the military convoy that had brought them from Sherman to Post 17. Four jeeps and ten trucks were aligned bumper to bumper.

Blade turned and observed the swirl of activity taking place in the vicinity of the sentry hut. Post 17 was being converted into a makeshift Command Center for the duration of the mission. General Reese stood near the hut, barking orders to the soldiers. A half-dozen troopers were installing a large console inside the hut, while five more worked at setting up a portable generator near the north wall. Machine-gun emplacements were being established 20 yards to the east and the west of Highway 289. Mortars were being placed along the west edge of the road. A lookout tower was being constructed on the east side of the sentry hut. All told, there were 84 men engaged in various tasks.

A youthful officer in camouflage fatigues, carrying an M-16 slung over his right shoulder, walked up to the giant and saluted. "My men and I are ready to leave whenever you are, sir."

"Call me Blade," the Warrior said. "And there's no need to salute me, Lieutenant Garber."

"Begging your pardon, sir, but you're my superior officer for the duration of the mission. General Reese told me to take my orders from you until further notice," Lieutenant Garber noted.

"Fine. Then my first order is for you to call me Blade."

"Yes, sir. Blade," Garber said, and smiled.

"When do we get this show on the road?" Hickok inquired.

"It's nine A.M. now. We'll leave in an hour," Blade informed them.

General Reese came over, rubbing his hands together excitedly, a gleam in his brown eyes. "This is the life!" he exclaimed.

"It is?" Blade responded.

"Damn straight! I love to get out in the field, to be on the front lines," General Reese declared. "Except for when I'm out inspecting our installations, I spend my time pushing papers at my desk in Denver."

The mention of the Civilized Zone capital prompted Blade to recall the brief layover there en route to Texas. The Hurricane had landed at Stapleton Airport, and President Toland had insisted on treating the Warriors to a snack while the VTOL was refueled. Later, Toland had stood on the runway and waved as the jet climbed into the blue sky.

"I despise pushing papers," Reese stressed.

Blade nodded absently. "I can understand why." He stared at the laboring soldiers, thinking of the six hours they had spent in Sherman while the general organized the convoy to convey them to Sentry Post 17.

"I just wish it was me going into Dallas," General Reese said. "I haven't been involved in any combat for five or six years."

"You can join us," Hickok offered. "Bring your whole Army along. The more, the merrier."

"The fewer we send in, the less risk we run of spreading the disease if indeed there is a plague," General Reese pointed out. "You'll be on your own."

"Figures," Hickok muttered.

"There's something I've been meaning to ask you," Blade mentioned.

"What?" the general responded.

"You told us that Sentry Post 17 and Post 19 were both struck. What happened to Post 18?"

"Good question," General Reese said. "We wondered about the same thing ourselves. Sentry Post 18 is located on a secondary road between Highway 289 and Interstate 35. Either the attackers weren't aware of its existence, or they deliberately only attacked 17 and 19."

"How many sentry posts do you have near Dallas?"

"There are five," General Reese answered, gazing at the metropolis. "There's one on Highway 75 and another on Highway 78. Both of them are east of here."

"And they weren't hit?"

"Nope."

Blade reflected for a moment, then glanced at the sentry hut. "How soon before the Command Center will be operational?"

"Forty-five minutes at the max," General Reese said.

"What happened to that machine gun you promised me?"

"Thanks for reminding me," General Reese replied. "I'll be right back." He hurried toward the parked trucks, directing a nearby noncom to accompany him.

"Why didn't you bring along one of the firearms from our Family armory?" Geronimo asked.

"Because the Family doesn't own a machine gun like the one I want to use," Blade said.

"Since when have you been finicky about your guns?" Hickok asked. "Your specialty is knives. And the way you shoot, you're lucky if you can hit the broad side of a barn with a bazooka at point-blank range."

"Aren't you exaggerating just a bit?" Blade responded with a smile.

"Just a mite," the gunman acknowledged. In addition to his Colt Python revolvers, Hickok had a Navy Arms Henry Carbine slung over his left shoulder. The 44-40, a reproduction of a rifle used in the days of the Wild West, was a favorite of his. For this mission the gunman had included a derringer in his personal arsenal—a four-shot C.O.P. .357 Magnum, five and a half inches in length, double-action, constructed of stainless steel with four barrels. The derringer was concealed in a small holster attached to his left wrist two inches from the edge of his buckskin shirtsleeve.

Geronimo was also armed to the teeth. The Arminius rode in its holster under his right arm, and the tomahawk was under his belt in his right hip. In a shoulder holster under his left arm was a Taurus Model 65, and in his right hand he held a Browning B-80 automatic shotgun. A bandolier filled with spare shells slanted across his stocky chest. "What's so special about this machine gun?" he asked Blade. "You've used machine guns before. I thought you were partial to the Commando Arms Carbine."

"I was," Blade admitted, "until I started using the M60 on my assignments for the Freedom Force. The M60 has more stopping power than the Commando. Comparing them is like comparing a slingshot to a cannon."

"I'll believe that when I see it," Hickok said.

"Excuse me, sir," Lieutenant Garber interjected. "I've used the M60 on a bipod on several occasions, and I think the gun is an excellent weapon."

"Brown-noser," Hickok mumbled.

"My only complaint is that the M60 is slightly difficult to control in the rapid-fire mode," Lieutenant Garber commented. "Don't you find it difficult to keep the bipod steady?"

"I don't use the bipod," Blade divulged.

"Do you use a tripod, sir?"

"No."

"Then how do you control the weapon?" Lieutenant Garber

asked, puzzled by the idea of anyone firing the M60 without a support. "Do you brace the stock against your hip in the conventional shooting posture?"

"I hold it in my hands."

"But that's impossible, sir," Lieutenant Garber said without thinking.

"Are you callin' my pard a liar?" Hickok demanded.

"Of course not," Lieutenant Garber replied.

"Good. We wouldn't want to lose a man before we start the mission," Hickok stated, and grinned impishly.

"All I meant was that it would be inconceivable for someone to fire the M60 like you would an ordinary machine gun," Lieutenant Garber elaborated. "You'd have to be as strong as an ox."

Before the others quite realized what he was doing, and before a stunned Lieutenant Garber could collect his wits, Blade stepped in close, gripped the front of the officer's shirt in his right hand, seized Garber's right thigh in his left hand, and hoisted the young lieutenant into the air.

"Sir!" Garber blurted.

Hickok cackled.

Geronimo stared quizzically at his giant companion.

"Is this strong enough for you?" Blade asked, smiling.

"Yes, sir!" Lieutenant Gaber cried.

Blade slowly lowered the officer to the road, his arm and shoulder muscles rippling. "I trust you won't see fit to doubt my word again?"

Lieutenant Garber licked his thin lips. "No, sir! I'll never doubt you again."

"Fine. This assignment will undoubtedly be extremely dangerous. I'll need your complete trust at all times."

"You have it, sir," Lieutenant Garber assured the Warrior.

"Okay. Go get your squad. I want to meet them," Blade directed.

"On my way," Garber said. He spun and hastened away.

"It's not like you to show off," Geronimo observed.

"I was making a point," Blade said.

"Sure," Geronimo said.

"Give Blade a break! He didn't hurt the greenhorn," Hickok said.

General Reese and the noncom were coming toward the Warriors. "What the hell was that all about?" the officer asked.

"I was getting my morning exercise," Blade quipped.

"Well, I've got your machine gun," General Reese said, and nodded at the noncom.

Hickok took one look and his eyes widened. "Wow! Now that's what I call a piece of hardware."

The M60E3 general-purpose machine gun had served as a versatile support weapon for the U.S. military for decades prior to the war. The Air Force had used the M60 for forward airfield defense and base security, while the Navy had used the M60 on their patrol craft and for their elite SEAL teams. Both the Army and the Marines utilized the M60 even more extensively. Modified versions had been employed on helicopter gunships and as helicopter door guns. The Marines had issued six M60's to each rifle company commander.

Each M60 was 42 inches in length and weighed almost 19 pounds. It used standard 7.62mm ammunition, and the gunner could select a mix of tracer, ball, and armor-piercing rounds. With a rate of 100 rounds per minute in the sustained mode, 200 in the rapid fire, and up to 650 cyclic, the M60 provided blistering firepower. Its effective range was well over a thousand yards.

The noncom held the big machine gun in both hands, and draped over his shoulders were two ammo belts. "Here you are, sir," he said.

Blade took the M60 and hefted the weapon, his lips curling upward. He leaned the machine gun against his legs and took the ammo belts, sliding each arm through one of the belts and angling the belts across his chest. "Thanks."

"Anything you want, you get," General Reese reponded.

"I want to travel light. We'll need six strips of jerky per man, canteens we can loop on the back of our belts, and a portable radio.''

"That's right. You prefer jerky over field rations. I'll dig some up. Give me ten minutes," Reese said, and walked toward the hut.

Blade lifted the M60 and saw Lieutenant Garber and four troopers approaching.

"Here's my squad, sir," Garber announced, saluting.

The quartet snapped to attention.

"Introduce me," Blade instructed.

Garber indicated each soldier with a wave of his left hand. All four were armed with M16's and a semiautomatic pistol. "This is Private Griffonetti, Private Humes, Private McGonical, and Private Liter."

"I'm Blade," the Warrior said, nodding at each man, appraising them. Griffonetti was swarthy and dark haired, Humes was a string bean, McGonical stocky and square jawed, and Liter possessed a sinewy build. "I'll expect all of you to follow my orders to the letter. Is that understood?"

A chorus of "Yes, sir!" punctuated his question.

"We'll be leaving shortly," Blade told them. "If you—" He stopped when he realized the four privates and Lieutenant Garber were all gazing past him, to the south, with amazement on their faces. He turned.

"Am I seein' what I think I'm seein'?" Hickok asked.

Blade wondered the same thing.

Approximately 100 yards from Sentry Post 17, in the middle of the road, were two women on horseback.

"They came out of the brush on the right," Geronimo said.

Both women had long hair. One rode a white horse, the other a black steed.

"Do I need my peepers examined, or are they buck naked?" Hickok queried in disbelief.

"They're nude," Geronimo verified.

"Maybe there's a shortage of clothes hereabouts," Hickok cracked.

Blade's eyes narrowed as he tried to distinguish details. The women were simply sitting there, watching the soldiers. Some of the troopers had noticed the two riders and ceased working to gawk in astonishment.

"Do you want me to go after them in a jeep?" Lieutenant Garber inquired eagerly.

"No," Blade said. "They'd just take to the brush and you wouldn't be able to catch them. For all we know, there might be more hiding in the fields or in those buildings, waiting to jump whoever goes after the women."

Hickok unslung his Henry. "Do you want me to wing one of them, pard? It'd be a piece of cake."

"Too risky," Blade said. "We need a prisoner intact."

General Reese rushed up. "It's them! It's them!"

"Who?" Hickok responded.

"The women I told you about," General Reese said, gesturing at the riders.

"What women? You must be sufferin' from heatstroke. All I see are two figments of your imagination."

"Figments of—!" General Reese blustered, and glanced at Blade. "Is he *always* this way?"

"Always," Blade said.

"How do you put up with it?"

Geronimo chuckled. "Don't let him get to you. All you have to do is remember you're dealing with a congenital idiot."

General Reese gazed at the women. "What do you suppose they're doing there?"

"Counting your men," Blade replied.

"What?" Reese exclaimed.

"What else would they be doing? They're memorizing the disposition of your forces."

"Damn!" General Reese fumed.

"I've got to hand it to him or her," Blade commented.

"Who?" General Reese asked.

"The brains behind their operation. The person in charge doesn't miss a trick. They must be monitoring your sentry posts constantly."

The two women abruptly rode into the undergrowth on the right side of Highway 289 and disppeared from view.

"Let them look all they want," General Reese stated. "They'll know we're ready for anything they throw at us."

"And that's not all," Blade remarked.

"What?"

Blade gazed at his fellow Warriors. "If they keep the sentry posts under constant surveillance, they'll know we're coming."

CHAPTER SEVEN

"I feel like a blamed sittin' duck."

"You're walking."

"Okay. I feel like a walkin' duck."

Geronimo snorted. "If you ask me, I think you've quacked," he said, and shook with repressed laughter.

"Pitiful. Just pitiful," Hickok muttered. "It's sad to see a body moseying around without a mind to direct it."

"So *that's* your problem," Geronimo said.

In front of them, Blade suddenly halted and glanced back. "I don't want to hear another peep out of you."

"What's the big deal?" Hickok countered. "They know we're comin' anyway."

"Most likely. But we don't need to compound the problem by advertising our presence," Blade said.

They were advancing southward on Highway 289, and they had reached a point about 200 yards from the sentry point. Blade came first in line, then Hickok and Geronimo, followed by Lieutenant Garber, and Humes, McGonical, Liter, and Griffonetti. The soldiers held their M-16's at the ready. Liter bore the radio on his back.

Blade scrutinized the field on the left, then studied the row of neglected, worn-down structures on the right. There was no sign of movement in the shadows. A hot breeze from the southwest caressed his cheeks. His instincts warned him that they were being watched, and he fingered the M60 trigger nervously. In a way, he hoped they would be attacked right then and there. Their mission was to capture an infected individual, and the sooner they accomplished their task, the sooner they could return to Sentry Post 17.

They passed the structures without incident.

Frowning, Blade scanned the terrain ahead, mentally marking the positions of the densest vegetation. Three hundred yards distant on the left, affording ample hiding places for unseen watchers, abandoned frame homes in various stages of disrepair were arranged in a tidy line stretching for as far as the eye could see. A former residential neighborhood, Blade deduced.

"Pssst! Can I peep?" Hickok whispered.

"What is it?" Blade said softly over his right shoulder.

"What were General Blood-and-Guts and you yakkin' about when we were gettin' set to leave? I heard him mention that private, Nelson."

"General Reese received a message from President Toland," Blade disclosed. "Private Nelson hasn't displayed any strange symptoms yet. No fever, no green splotches. He appears to be in excellent health."

"So maybe the green splotches aren't contagious," Hickok stated hopefully.

"It's too soon to tell."

"Boy, are you a bundle of sunshine."

They proceeded warily, drawing ever nearer to the frame houses. The undergrowth was deathly still; not so much as a bug buzzed.

"I've got a bad feeling about this," Hickok commented.

Blade heard a twig snap to his right and pivoted, leveling the M60, and glimpsed a hunched-over figure scurrying through the brush. The figure promptly dropped from sight. Blade raised his left hand and pumped his arm twice, and instantly Hickok and Geronimo flanked him.

"I saw it," Geronimo said.

"So did I, pard," Hickok stated.

They waited for a full minute but nothing happened.

"What's going on?" Lieutenant Garber inquired, joining them and peering at the undergrowth in confusion. "Why have you stopped?"

"Were you daydreamin'?" Hickok rejoined.

"We're being shadowed," Blade revealed.

"What? Where?" Lieutenant Garber asked, gazing all around.

"Don't pee your pants, junior," Hickok said. "They're not aimin' to attack us yet."

"How do you know?" Garber questioned skeptically.

"If they intended to kill and us keep us from entering their territory, they would have charged us already," Blade speculated. "They might want us alive. If so, they'll wait to jump us until we're out of hearing range of Sentry Post 17."

"If you're certain they plan to attack us, why don't we go back and try again after dark?" Lieutenant Garber proposed.

"It wouldn't make any difference," Blade said. "If they're watching the sentry post around the clock, they'd see us enter at night." He paused. "No, we go in now. At least we have the daylight in our favor. They can't come at us without being spotted."

"We hope," Hickok said.

Blade straightened and waved his left arm forward. "Stay frosty," he advised, and led the way.

"In this heat?" Hickok complained. "You must be kiddin'."

"There would be a lot less hot air if you'd keep your trap shut for five minutes," Geronimo joked.

"At least I don't fart folks to death," Hickok retorted.

"And I do?"

"Who ate that moldy can of baked beans we found that time?" Hickok stated. "Who went around fartin' up a storm for a week? Who wilted plants at ten feet? Who got jumped by a female skunk that mistook him for a male polecat?"

"Rikki-Tikki-Tavi?"

"Try again, rocks-for-brains."

"What can I say? That took place twelve years ago. And I wasn't jumped by a female skunk," Geronimo said.

"You mean that smell was your *natural* odor?" Hickok asked, and smirked in triumph.

"Children, please," Blade said sternly.

They fell silent.

An hour went by and on they trekked through the residential suburb of the city. The buildings had all sustained weather-related damage during the 106 years since the nuclear Armageddon. Roofs were blistered and broken and partly caved in in many cases. The exterior walls were cracked and crumbling. Hardly a window was intact.

"Do you reckon the people who lived here skedaddled when the war broke out?" Hickok asked.

"Most of them, anyway," Blade answered. "We know the U.S. government evacuated hundreds of thousands, maybe more, into the Rocky Mountain region and the Midwest at the onset of hostilities."

"I wonder why the lousy Commies didn't hit Dallas with a nuclear bomb or missile?"

"Who knows? Their systems weren't very accurate. Maybe they tried and missed. Maybe there were other targets they wanted to take out first. General Reese told me that Dallas was rated as a tertiary target," Blade said.

"Terry who?"

"Dallas wasn't considered crucial by the Soviets."

"If I was from Dallas, I'd be plumb insulted," Hickok commented.

"So would the—" Geronimo froze in midstride. He tilted his head.

"What is it?" Hickok asked.

Blade halted and surveyed their surroundings. Decayed, disintegrating homes were on both sides of the highway. Forty feet in front of them on the left, rearing six stories into the humid air, rose a squat black structure. Large, faded words were visible near the top, with several letters missing. Blade read the letters.

W-R-D —NK.

"I heard a sound," Geronimo announced.

"What kind of sound?" Blade inquired. He'd learned to rely upon the exceptional senses Geronimo possessed. Undoubtedly because of his Blackfoot inheritance, Geronimo enjoyed outstanding eyesight and hearing.

"A hissing, like something expelling a breath," Geronimo stated.

"Are you sure you weren't fartin' again?" Hickok asked.

Blade advanced cautiously, his eyes scrutinizing the nearby homes and settling on the black monolith. The building had been constructed of an opaque, glasslike substance. All of the upper four floors were intact, but there were gaping holes in the two lower stories, gloomy, ragged cavities averaging five feet in diameter. What could have made those holes? he wondered. Looters? Scavengers? An explosion of some kind?

A faint scraping noise came from the monolith.

Blade swung the M60 to cover the monolith. He detected a flicker of movement in a cavity on the southwest corner, a brief streak of a thin, reddish whip.

What in the world?

He tread lightly, striving to peer into the murky recesses of the artificial caves. Were the attackers lurking within, girding for a charge? He came abreast of the monolith, his body tensed for action, ready for anything.

Or so he thought.

A huge reptilian head suddenly poked from a cavity on the ground floor, its red tongue darting in and out of its wicked-looking maw. The skin was a rusty brown with distinct, rough scales. Its dark, unfathomable eyes were enclosed in rings of bright red. The beast stood at least five feet high at the shoulders.

"Dear Lord!" Lieutenant Garber exclaimed.

More reptilian creatures appeared, glaring balefully at the humans, their demeanor unmistakably menacing.

"Why do I feel like a slab of venison?" Hickok quipped.

Blade continued walking slowly, hoping they could pass the monolith without incident.

"I didn't know there were alligators in Texas," Hickok said.

"Those aren't alligators, you dummy. They're mutations. Spiny lizards, I believe," Geronimo stated.

"No foolin', professor?"

Nine lizards were now staring at the Warriors and soldiers.

"Do you suppose they eat things like insects and snakes?" Hickok asked of no one in particular.

"We should be so lucky," Geronimo responded.

One of the larger lizards abruptly sprang from its hole, darting at its intended prey with astounding speed, legs flying, mouth wide open. As if on cue, all the rest of the mutations burst from their dens, swooping toward the highway en masse.

"Here they come!" Lieutenant Garber belabored the obvious.

The first lizard made a beeline at Hickok.

"Eat this, sucker!" the gunman declared, the Henry already to his right shoulder. The rifle boomed.

The shot caught the reptile in the mouth, the slug boring through its head and tearing out the top of its cranium. It stumbled and sprawled onto its bluish-tinged belly, thrashing uncontrollably.

Geronimo cut loose with the Browning, and the chatter of M-16's created a metallic din as the Civilized Zone troopers opened up.

Move! Blade's mind shrieked, and he did, taking several strides to the east, wanting the angle to be just right so he wouldn't accidentally hit any of his friends and allies. The short span of grass between the monolith and the curb was a mass of hurtling mutations. He squeezed the trigger, gripping the M60 firmly with both hands, his legs braced.

A hail of rounds slammed into the closest lizard, bowling the beast over, miniature geysers spraying from its perforated body.

Blade elevated the barrel, going for the next two creatures, seeing his slugs rip into their heads and necks, the M60 thundering and bucking.

Hickok and Geronimo were pouring lead into another of the genetic deviates.

The remaining four lizards surged toward the soldiers. Despite the deadly rain from the M-16's, they barely checked their rush. A bulky mutant reached Humes and struck, clamping its jaws on the trooper's midriff and lifting him from the ground. Humes screamed as the lizard shook him savagely. He dropped his M-16 and flailed ineffectually at the lizard's head.

Private McGonical emptied his magazine into a charging monstrosity, and the creature fell dead almost at his feet.

Backpedaling frantically, Private Liter fired at an onrushing lizard. His rounds punched into its head, staggering the thing for an instant, and then the mutation lunged, its jaws smacking shut on Liter's head. Liter screeched and attempted to ram the M-16 into the lizard's throat, but the creature whipped its head from side to side, swinging Liter as if he was a mere stick. On the sixth swing there came a loud snap, then a squishy, ripping noise, and Liter's headless body flopped to the roadway, blood gushing from the severed neck. The lizard swallowed, gulped, and blinked.

Lieutenant Garber and Private McGonical fired into the creature holding Humes, and the beast promptly dropped on the spot.

The last two mutations were both after Griffonetti, who had whirled and raced behind a tree on the opposite side of the highway. Keeping the trunk between himself and the lizards, he had managed to evade their snapping jaws while firing repeatedly into their heads. But now his M-16 went empty at the moment the creatures came at him from different directions.

Griffonetti, his fingers fumbling as he tried to insert a fresh magazine, panic-stricken at the sight of the two lizards coming at him, thought he was doomed. Out of the corner of his right eye he saw someone racing toward him, and then Blade materialized with the M60 pouring forth death and destruction. The first lizard went down, convulsing, and the second twisted as a dozen rounds penetrated its left side. It scrambled at the Warrior, only to have its head be stitched from crown to mouth. Gurgling obscenely, the beast fell.

The sudden silence seemed eerie.

Blade scanned the dead and dying lizards, insuring none of them were capable of inflicting any harm. He spotted Liter's corpse and walked over, scowling in disgust. The body lay on its back, blood still pumping from the neck. Blade knelt and rolled the corpse over, then opened the backpack containing their radio, expecting to find the worst. He did.

Loose wires protruded from the cracked casing.

"Private Humes is dead," Lieutenant Garber declared, walking over, his face ashen.

"Two men dead and we're not even to the downtown section yet!" Blade snapped.

"Do you think there are more of those things around?" Lieutenant Garber asked, glancing at the monolith.

"There might be," Blade said. "See if you can make this radio work." He rose and joined Hickok and Geronimo, who were standing near the curb and eyeing the black building.

"We saw something move in there, pard," the gunfighter said.

"We should keep moving," Geronimo suggested.

"I know," Blade said.

"Everybody and their grandmother will know we're in Dallas now," Hickok said.

"I know," Blade responded again, his tone bitter.

"What's eatin' you?" Hickok inquired.

"As usual, everything is going wrong from the start," Blade replied.

"Murphy's Law," Geronimo said.

Blade frowned. "Just once I'd like a mission to go exactly as planned."

"Remember what the Elders say," Geronimo observed. "Hardship breeds character."

"Then we should have more character than we'll know what

to do with by the time this run is over," Blade said.

Hickok and Geronimo looked at one another.

"I want both of you to play it safe," Blade directed. "Especially you, Hickok. You have a knack for getting into trouble."

"Who, me?" the gunman responded.

"I'm serious," Blade said. "I don't want to lose another man. Not Garber or his men, and certainly not either of you."

"The same goes for you," Geronimo stated.

"We'll cover your back all the way," Hickok offered.

Lieutenant Garber, Private McGonical, and Private Griffonetti approached.

"The radio is shot," the officer said.

"Figures," Blade muttered.

"We'll be ready to leave after we bury Humes and Liter," Lieutenant Garber said.

"Forget it."

"Sir?"

"We can't afford to waste time burying our dead," Blade stated. "We keep going. I'm sorry."

Garber, Griffonetti, and McGonical looked at one another.

"Begging your pardon, sir, but we don't think it's right to go off and leave their bodies to be consumed by the wild animals and the mutations," Lieutenant Garber commented.

Blade sighed. "I repeat. We can't take the time to bury Humes and Liter. Grab their weapons, spare ammo, and their personal effects and let's go."

"But—" Lieutenant Garber started to protest.

"Didn't General Reese tell you to follow my orders explicitly?" Blade asked sharply, cutting him off.

"Yes, sir," Garber dutifully replied.

"Then you'll do as I say or I'll report you when we get back," Blade promised. "Collect the M-16's, the pistols, and their personal effects *now*!"

Reluctantly, their expressions downcast, the three soldiers went to comply.

"Garber doesn't have a thing to worry about," Hickok

remarked.

"How do you figure?" Blade asked.

"You threatened to put him on report when we get back," the gunfighter noted.

"So?"

"So it's more like *if* we get back."

CHAPTER EIGHT

Once a teeming, thriving hub of commerce and industry, a vibrant metropolis throbbing with the pulsebeat of millions, Dallas now resembled the majority of decrepit, forsaken cities and towns dotting the postwar countryside. The hot breeze stirred the dust that caked the streets and buildings. Broken bits of glass lay under every window. Trash and debris littered the sidewalks and avenues. The rusted hulks of cars and trucks bore testimony to the American mania for owning private vehicles. Trash and garbage were piled in the alleys. Reeking waste matter provided a breeding ground for noxious insects. Feral dogs and cats prowled restlessly, and rats and other vile vermin skittered in the shadows.

"I wish I'd brought a clothespin," Hickok mentioned.

"What for?" Blade asked.

"To pinch my nose shut. This place stinks worse than Geronimo's farts."

"Will you stop with the farts already," Geronimo declared.

Blade held up his right hand, bringing them to a halt. From his right front pants pocket he extracted the map General Reese had given him. He opened the map and placed it on the cracked and pitted asphalt.

"Where the dickens are we?" Hickok inquired.

"I'll know in a minute," Blade said.

"Did you see that sign back there at that joint with the red roof?" Hickok asked.

"What about it?" Geronimo interjected.

"What did that sign mean? What's pizza? We've run into a lot of pizza signs in some of the other cities we've been to," Hickok said.

"I can answer that," Lieutenant Garber spoke up. "We still have pizza in the Civilized Zones. It's usually a flat, circular pie or crust topped with cheese, pepperoni, hamburger, you name it. My favorite topping is anchovies."

"What are anchovies?" Hickok asked.

"Little fish."

Hickok snorted. "Fish pies. Give me apple or cherry any day."

"Here we are," Blade declared, tapping the map. "We're at the junction of Highway 289 and Forest Lane. We'll take a right on Forest Lane and work our way into the inner city." He paused. "I'm surprised we haven't run into the ones we're after yet. Maybe they're waiting for the right moment to strike." He folded the map and replaced it in his pocket, then looked at Lieutenant Garber, who was still clearly upset over not being permitted to bury the two troopers. "Move out," he said, motioning with his right arm.

They hiked west on Forest Lane, then turned south on Midway Road.

Blade felt disappointed by the lack of hostile activity. His plan to take a prisoner and vacate Dallas quickly was being thwarted by the refusal of those bearing the splotches to show themselves. They undoubtedly had a headquarters hidden somewhere in the city, and he racked his mind for a strategy that would lure them into exposing themselves.

An alley appeared on the right.

Blade stared at the heaps of refuse lining the alley entrance, an obvious indication that a large number of people were using the area on a regular basis, and frowned in disappointment. He took two more steps, then halted and whirled when a shuffling noise came from beyond the mounds of filth.

Footsteps pattered.

Blade pointed at Hickok, then the alley, and together they sprinted into its depths, skirting the fetid piles. The towering buildings on both sides obscured the high afternoon sun. He almost gagged at the stench, and to compensate he breathed shallowly as he ran.

Up ahead something moved.

Something on two legs.

"Stop!" Blade cried. He saw a frightened face glance at him, and the figure moved faster. "We won't harm you!"

Whoever it was didn't believe him. The figure ran recklessly, and that haste proved a mistake. Evidently the figure slipped on the garbage, because the next second there was a terrified squeal, a flapping of arms, and a loud crash as the runner went down, headfirst, into a rubbish heap less than six yards from a ten-foot-high wall.

Blade and Hickok slowed, covering their quarry.

"Don't move!" Blade ordered.

The runner ignored the command, slipping and sliding in the mushy garbage while trying to rise.

Blade glimpsed long, stringy black hair and grimy feminine features, and he realized they had chased a young woman.

"Don't kill me!" she wailed.

"We won't hurt you," Blade told her.

She twisted to confront them, her fear conveyed in the set of her countenance, her brown eyes wide. Her clothes were little better than rags, a green shirt and brown pants, both faded and torn in a dozen spots, both coated with bits of foul, slimy, clinging refuse. The only marks on her face were smudges of dirt.

"It's just a blamed girl!" Hickok exclaimed.

"Who are you calling a girl?" she demanded, an incipient arrogance supplanting her fright.

"You," Hickok responded, "although it's hard to tell under all that gunk."

She studied them for a moment, then looked down at herself and whined. "Look at what you made me do!"

"We didn't make you do nothin'," Hickok said. "It's not our fault you're a klutz."

"I'm not a klutz, you meathead!" she snapped.

"You're the one wearin' garbage," Hickok reminded her.

"Up yours!"

Hickok glanced at Blade and laughed. "Friendly wench, isn't she?"

"I'm not a wench!" she declared. "Whatever that is."

"A wench is a woman who doesn't know she's a lady," Hickok said confidently.

"I'm a lady, you prick!" she informed them. "Who are you? Why the hell were you after me? You don't look like you're with the Chains or the Stompers, and you sure as hell ain't one of the Chosen."

"We'll ask the questions," Blade stated.

"And what if I don't want to answer?"

Blade squatted and stared into her eyes. "I need information, and you're the one who can supply it. You'll tell us what we want to know, one way or the other."

"You don't scare me!" she said defiantly.

"What's your name?" Blade inquired.

"Get stuffed."

"Suit yourself," Blade said, and looked at Hickok. "Shoot her in the leg."

"The right or the left one?" the gunman responded.

"Take your pick."

The woman glanced from one to the other in consternation. "You're bluffing! You wouldn't shoot me!"

Blade nodded. "You're right. I wouldn't shoot you." He pointed at the gunfighter. "But he will."

"The Henry would be a mite noisy in this alley," Hickok commented, and slowly drew his right Python. "I'll try to miss the bone," he assured her, cocking the hammer. With deliberate care he aimed at her right leg.

She licked her full lips and swallowed hard. "Now hold on a second!"

"I just hope I don't hit an artery or a vein," Hickok mentioned. "If you lose a lot of blood you might get a tad dizzy."

"Wait! Wait!" she shouted, holding her arms up. "Don't do anything I'll regret!"

"Sorry," Hickok said, and shrugged. "Nothin' personal."

"Don't shoot!" she cried, and glanced at Blade. "I'll talk! I'll talk! I think that son of a bitch would really plug me."

Hickok smiled and twirled the Colt into its holster.

"What's your name?" Blade repeated.

"Melanie Stevens."

"How old are you?"

"What's my age got to do with anything?" Melanie asked.

Blade sighed and gazed at the gunman. "It looks like you'll have to shoot her after all."

"Fine by me."

Melanie shook her hands from side to side. "No! No! No! I'm nineteen! Nineteen!"

"How long have you lived in Dallas?" Blade questioned.

"In this city? About a year."

"Where did you live before that?"

"I drifted around a lot," Melanie said.

"Where's your family?"

Melanie did a double take. "My what?"

"Your mother and father. Your brothers and sisters," Blade said.

"My mom kicked the bucket when I was four and my dad was killed by a gang in Texarkana when I was twelve. I don't have any brothers or sisters."

Blade straightened and offered her his left hand.

Surprise flitted across her features and she hesitated before taking hold and allowing herself to be pulled erect. "Thanks, mister. It's nice to know that at least *one* of you can be a gentleman when he wants to."

"My name is Blade," he disclosed. "This is Hickok."

"Howdy, ma'am," the gunfighter said.

"Ma'am?"

"Never mind him," Blade directed her. "It sounds to me like you've spent your entire life in the Outlands."

"Where else would I live?" Melanie responded, puzzled

by the query.

"Why didn't your family head north and live in the Civilized Zone? You'd be safer there than wandering around the Outlands," Blade pointed out.

"The Civilized Zone?" Melanie said, and snorted. "My dad told me all about that place. They have guard posts everywhere, and if you try to sneak across their border the guards will shoot you."

"They have sentry posts," Blade admitted, "but the sentries don't shoot travelers on sight. They detain those who want to enter the Civilized Zone until identities are established and physicals are administered, but they don't shoot without provocation."

"All I know is what my dad told me," Melanie said. "And he told me they shoot on sight."

Blade was about to refute her when he abruptly recalled a pertinent fact. "Wait a minute. Years ago a dictator by the name of Samuel the Second ruled the Civilized Zone, and he had thousands upon thousands slain in cold blood. But Samuel was killed about six years ago."

"Oh, yeah? How do you know he's really dead?"

"I killed him."

Melanie blinked a few times, her brow creasing in bewilderment. "You took old Sammy out?"

Blade nodded.

"Hmmph. I guess the rumors I heard were true, but I wasn't about to try and find out by waltzing up to a guard post and having my head shot off."

"You'd prefer to live like an animal, wandering from town to town, never having enough to eat, never having a place you can call home?"

"Hey, I do whatever it takes to survive," Melanie said defensively.

Blade absently stroked his chin, regarding her critically. "Okay. Tell me about Dallas."

"What do you want to know?"

"Everything. You mentioned the Chains and the Stompers. Who are they?" Blade probed.

"They were the top gangs until the Chosen came along. The Chains claimed the northern half of the city as their turf, and the Stompers had the southern half."

"The Chains and the Stompers are street gangs?"

"Isn't that what I just said?"

"Do they still control their . . . turf?" Blade asked.

"Nope. The Chosen have taken over the whole damn city. Oh, there are still Chains and Stompers left, but there are fewer and fewer every week. In another year the Chosen will be the only ones in Dallas, which is how they want it," Melanie explained.

"Who are the Chosen?"

Melanie shuddered and gazed around nervously. "The freakiest bunch you'd ever want to meet."

"Freaky?"

"They have these green marks all over their bodies," Melanie said.

Blade gripped her right shoulder. "Marks? Do you mean they have green splotches?"

"Marks. Splotches. What's the diff? You'd best stay away from those suckers or your ass is grass."

"They're the ones we're looking for," Blade said, releasing her.

"Let me get this straight," Melanie stated, sounding stunned. "You're *looking* for the Chosen? You *want* to find them?"

"Yes."

"You're wacko."

Blade glanced toward the mouth of the alley and spied Geronimo standing in the entrance, watching them. "I want you to take us to them."

"Take you to the Chosen?" Melanie declared, her left hand rising to her throat.

"Right now."

"No way."

Blade shifted the M60 from his left hand to his right. "Why not?"

"Don't you have ears? If the Chosen find you, you're

history. If you don't have the Mark, then they'll give it to you or waste your ass," Melanie said.

"They can give the green marks to those who don't have them?"

"So I've been told," Melanie replied.

"The blasted disease must be contagious," Hickok interjected.

"We knew the possibility existed before we came to Dallas," Blade mentioned.

"Sherry will clobber me if I get green splotches all over my body," Hickok groused. "She reckons I'm perfect the way I am."

"Demented?"

"Now don't you start, pard. I take enough insults from Geronimo."

Blade motioned at the alley entrance. "You're coming with us," he informed Melanie.

"Where to?"

"To the Chosen."

She retreated a step, shaking her head. "Not on your life. I'm not committing suicide for you or anyone else."

"We'll protect you," Blade pledged.

"You racked Sammy so you must be hot stuff, but you don't have any idea of what you're up against here. There must be a hundred and fifty of the Chosen. The two of you wouldn't stand a chance."

"There are others with us."

"How many? Fifty? Sixty?"

"There are four more," Blade said.

"Six against the Chosen?" Melanie stated, and snickered. "They'll wipe you out, or worse."

"What could be worse?" Blade questioned.

"They could convert you."

"How do they con—" Blade checked his sentence when he heard a blast of gunfire erupt in the street. "We need her! Bring her!" he ordered the gunfighter, and raced for the alley entrance.

CHAPTER NINE

Blade burst from the alley to find a battle being waged.

Geronimo, Lieutenant Garber, Private Griffonetti, and Private McGonical were under assault from dozens of assailants. Grungy figures lined the roofs, were framed in windows, or had taken cover behind every available shelter.

Blade saw a tall black man on the roof across the street let fly with an arrow from a compound bow. The shaft sped true, slicing into Griffonetti's throat and protruding out the back of his neck. Griffonetti clutched at the arrow, his M-16 clattering on the asphalt, and he dropped to his knees. Without a moment's hesitation, Blade angled the M60 upward and squeezed the trigger. The heavy slugs tore into the assailant and catapulted him from sight.

A man and a woman were charging from the right, each with a chain looped around their waist, each armed with a sword.

Blade pivoted, lowering the machine gun's barrel, and sent several rounds into each foe. They were flung to the road on their backs, kicking and shaking in their death throes.

A chunk of brick struck Blade on the right temple, filling his head with excruciating pain, and he twisted and glanced up to discover a man with a beard in a second-floor window, about to hurl a bigger piece of brick. Blade gritted his teeth and fired, and the man screeched as he staggered backwards and vanished.

Griffonetti had pitched onto his stomach.

A burly man in a leather jacket appeared at a ground-floor window in a building on the other side of the street, a rifle in his hands. He got off a shot.

Private McGonical took the bullet squarely in the chest. He looked down at the wound in astonishment, then sprawled forward.

Geronimo worked the Browning, three booming retorts one after the other, and the rifleman's waist exploded outward and he crumpled.

The figures were aiming a torrent of bullets, spears, arrows, bricks, and other items at the exposed Warriors and Lieutenant Garber.

"Into the alley!" Blade yelled, sweeping the M60 in an arc, forcing their adversaries to duck or die.

Geronimo and Lieutenant Garber darted into the mouth of the alley, then fired to keep the enemy pinned down while Blade joined them.

The downpour of missiles and lead ceased.

"What happened?" Blade asked, scanning the buildings and roofs. "Who were they?"

"Your guess is as good as mine," Geronimo answered. "One second we were waiting for you, and the next they popped out of nowhere, trying to kill us."

"All my men are dead," Garber said sadly. "I never expected this!"

"Concentrate on staying alive yourself," Blade advised, and risked a peek past the edge of the right-hand wall. There was no hint of movement. "They seem to be gone."

As if on cue, a gruff voice hailed them from atop the three-story structure directly across from the alley. "Hey, you! The big son of a bitch! Do you hear me?"

"I hear you!" Blade replied, vigiantly scrutinizing the rim of the roof.

"You ain't getting out of there alive, you scum-bag!"

Blade did not bother to respond.

"Who are you?" the man asked. "Are you hooked up with the Stompers?"

Still Blade said nothing. He leaned his back against the wall and waited.

"Look, man! I want to talk to you face to face. What do you say?"

"Come out into the middle of the street, unarmed," Blade shouted.

"Unarmed? No frigging way!"

Blade glanced at Geronimo, who was reloading the Browning, and at Lieutenant Garber, who seemed to be extremely depressed.

"How about this idea?" the man on the roof yelled. "How about if my hands are empty but I pack my revolvers? You can bring that cannon of yours. What do you say?"

"Keep your hands where I can see them!" Blade instructed.

Silence descended for a full minute, until the peeling, chipped wooden door in the building on the other side of the street opened and out walked a lean man attired in a brown leather vest and baggy black pants. His left boot had a wide hole at the tip, exposing three toes. Around his waist were belted a pair of Taurus Model 66's. Also looped about his body, inches above the revolvers, was a length of chain. He came forward slowly, his brown eyes fixed on the alley, his arms held out from his sides.

"Watch my back," Blade ordered, and stepped out to meet the spokesman for their adversaries. He surveyed the street and the buildings, and although no one was in sight he knew weapons were being trained on him.

The man glanced at the M60. "That's the biggest damn gun I've ever seen, mister."

Blade judged the spokesman to be in his early twenties. Under the dirt and the grime was a frank, earnest face. "What do you want?" he demanded harshly.

"Hey, chill out," the man said. "I'm here under a truce. I'm doing you a favor."

"How do you figure?"

"I'm giving you a chance to get out of this alive," the man stated.

Blade's mouth curled upwards. "I'd get out of this alive, with or without your generosity."

"Tough sucker, huh?"

"Get to the point."

The man wagged his hands. "Can I lower my arms?"

"No."

A grin creased the man's countenance. "Yep. Definitely a tough mother. Listen, there's no sense in us getting mad at each other. I'm not here to razz you. My name is Marlon," he said, and paused, staring at Blade expectantly. When he didn't receive a reply, he shrugged. "I'm the head of the Chains."

"Who cares?"

"Geez. Why are you being such a hard-ass?"

"You attacked us without warning and killed two of my team. What do you expect?" Blade retorted.

"Hey, you're the ones who invaded our turf and jumped my squeeze," Marlon said angrily.

"Your turf?"

"This part of the city belongs to the Chains, and no one enters our territory without permission," Marlon declared.

"That's strange. I was told that the Chains don't control any turf, that the Chosen rule Dallas."

"Who was the rotten, lying prick who told you that?"

Blade motioned at the alley. "A woman named Melanie."

"Is she all right?" Marlon inquired, trying to speak in a level, calm tone, but with a trace of anxiousness tinging his voice.

"She could use a bath," Blade mentioned.

"Who couldn't? Don't be insulting my squeeze, man," Marlon snapped.

"Is she your wife?"

"Wife, hell. She's my fox, my woman. She was out with Annie, scrounging for food, when they saw you and your buddies coming. Melanie ducked into the alley and Annie hid in an old store a few doors down. She saw you go after Melanie and snuck off to tell us," Marlon detailed. "Why'd you chase her? What did you do to her?"

"She's fine," Blade said. "We needed information. That was all."

Marlon cocked his head, his eyes narrowing. "You didn't have another reason, like maybe you wanted to get your paws on her body?"

Blade's features hardened. "How would you like to eat your teeth?"

Surprise registered on Marlon's face, and he regarded the giant carefully. "No, I guess you don't seem like the raping type. But how was I to know?"

"You ambushed us because you wanted to rescue Melanie?" Blade asked.

Marlon nodded. "Release her and we'll let you leave."

"No."

"Why the hell not?"

"I don't trust you," Blade said bluntly.

"But I give you my word," Marlon stated.

"It's not enough."

Forgetting himself for a moment, incensed by the Warrior's attitude, Marlon placed his hands on his hips. "Listen, jerk-face! When I give my word, I mean it. All I want is Melanie. Let her go and you're free."

"I want more than your word," Blade said.

"Like what?"

"I want you to agree to lead us to the Chosen."

The request shocked the head of the Chains. He gawked for a full five seconds before composing himself enough to blurt a response. "Say *what*?"

"You must know where the Chosen are based."

"Yeah. Sure. But I'm not about to lead you there."

"You will if you want us to release Melanie," Blade said.

"Do you have a death wish or something? Do you know who the Chosen are?" Marlon asked testily.

"Enlighten me."

"They're crazies, man. They all have these green spots on their skin, and they run around trying to convert everybody. Their head honcho is a mental case called the Lawgiver," Marlon said.

"Do they have a headquarters, somewhere they operate from?" Blade probed.

"Yeah."

"Then take us there."

Marlon pondered for half a minute, glancing repeatedly at the alley. "Let me get this straight. I agree to take you to the base of those damn wackos, and you'll let Melanie go?"

Blade nodded.

"How do I know she's okay? How do I know you ain't already offed her?"

"You can see for yourself," Blade suggested, and stepped aside. "After you."

The leader of the Chains frowned, torn between his desire to ascertain if the woman he loved was safe and his distrust of the giant. He tilted his head back and raised his voice. "I'm going to check on Melanie! Everything is cool! No one does anything until you hear from me!"

"Are you sure they heard you?" Blade asked.

"They heard me," Marlon said, and stalked toward the alley.

Blade followed, walking backwards, his eyes roving over the buildings. He spied a shadowy form in a second-floor window off to the left, but the Chains heeded their top man and not one bullet or arrow was fired.

"So where is she?" Marlon demanded, halting in the entrance and staring suspiciously at Geronimo and Lieutenant Garber.

"Where's Hickok?" Blade inquired, stopping next to his fellow Warrior.

"We haven't seen him since he entered the alley with you," Geronimo said.

"What?" Blade declared, and only then did he realize he

hadn't seen the gunman either, not since they had heard the gunshots.

"I just assumed you told him to stay with her at the back of the alley," Geronimo remarked.

"He was supposed to bring her out here," Blade said.

"Knowing that dummy, he probably got lost," Geronimo joked.

"Even Nathan can't get lost in an alley," Blade responded, starting into its depths.

"I wouldn't put anything past that idiot," Geronimo said.

"Hold it!" Marlon barked.

The Warriors drew up short.

"What the hell kind of game are you playing with me?" Marlon snapped.

"This isn't a game," Blade said.

"I think you're trying to sucker me back there so you can bump me off," Marlon said.

"Then stay here," Blade said, and looked at the officer. "Come with us."

The three of them hastened toward the rear of the alley.

Marlon watched them cover a dozen yards, then scowled and smacked his right fist into his left palm in frustration. He walked after them.

"Hickok!" Blade called.

"Yo, stupid!" Geronimo added.

Blade couldn't understand the gunfighter's absence. Melanie could never have overpowered Hickok, and if the gunman had been attacked by others there would have been the sound of shots. He jogged forward, avoiding the piles of trash, searching the recesses for his friend. "Where can he be?" he asked, an indefinite misgiving gnawing at his consciousness.

"I don't see him," Geronimo said apprehensively.

They came to the spot where the woman had slipped and fallen. There, prominently defined in the muck, were her footprints and those of the gunman and Blade.

Geronimo crouched and examined the prints.

"Is this where you left her?" Marlon inquired, catching up

to them.

"This is the spot," Blade said, watching Geronimo examine the ground diligently.

"Then where is she?" Marlon asked.

"You tell us."

Marlon gazed at the mounds of refuse. "You could have killed her and dumped her body in the garbage."

Pivoting on his right heel, Blade swung the M60 around and pointed the barrel at Marlon's chest. "Drop your guns," he commanded softly.

"What?" Marlon blurted out, flabbergasted.

"You heard me."

Breath hissed out of Marlon and he clenched his hands until the knuckles paled. "You lying, double-crossing scum!"

"Use your thumb and little finger on each hand, and *only* your thumb and little finger, and lift out each revolver," Blade directed, ignoring the insult. "Set the guns down on the ground very, very slowly."

"If you shoot me, turkey, the Chains will be on you like dogs on a bone," Marlon predicted.

"Let them come."

"You're bluffing," Marlon asserted.

"It's obvious Melanie and you were made for each other," Blade remarked.

"Huh?"

Blade tensed his arms. "Never mind. Drop your guns! Now!"

Fury contorted Marlon's face, and for the space of five seconds he gave the impression he was about to go for his guns. Scarlet infused his cheeks and his mouth worked noiselessly. Finally he obeyed, his hands shaking so badly from suppressed rage he could barely hold the revolvers as he lowered them. "If it's the last thing I ever do," he vowed when both handguns were on the ground, "I'm taking you out."

"No thanks. I'm married."

Marlon's brow knit in utter confusion.

"Pick up his guns," Blade told Lieutenant Garber. "Stick them under your belt, then cover him. He's not to get them back until I give the word."

"Get them back?" both Garber and Marlon said simultaneously.

"There must be an echo in here," Blade said.

"Do you really intend to give this bastard his guns back?" Lieutenant Garber asked as he squatted and retrieved the revolvers.

"In due course."

Garber straightened and stepped a yard away from the head of the Chains. He tucked the Taurus Model 66's under his belt and aimed his M-16 at Marlon's chest. "He's responsible for the deaths of McGonical and Griffonetti. He deserves to be shot."

"He wasn't the one who killed them," Blade noted.

"But I heard him say he's their leader. He might as well have fired the shot," Lieutenant Garber complained.

"You're not to shoot him unless he tries to grab his guns. Is that understood?" Blade queried.

"Yes."

"Yes, what?"

"Yes, *sir*."

Marlon looked at the Warrior quizzically and shook his head. "I don't get you, man. One minute you say one thing, and the next something else."

"Do I?"

"You're a space cadet," Marlon stated.

"Am I?" Blade responded, and turned toward Geronimo.

Bent over at the waist, his keen eyes riveted on the tracks, the stocky Warrior was reading the spoor as unerringly as he would the freshly imprinted trail of a bear or a doe. He had moved close to a shoulder-high stack of moldly, sagging cardboard boxes piled in the northwest corner.

"Hey! Wait a minute!" Marlon declared, snapping his fingers. "Maybe I do get you. You've been playing mind games with me."

"Have I?"

Geronimo stepped almost to the rear wall and gazed to his right. "Blade."

"What did you find?" Blade inquired, walking over.

"See for yourself," Geronimo said.

Blade did, and he resisted an urge to kick the cardboard boxes to vent his supreme vexation. For there, in the corner, concealed by the stack of boxes, was an open metal door leading into a gloomy corridor.

CHAPTER TEN

Hickok instinctively rotated toward the street as the gunfire boomed, raising the Henry, and he heard Blade yell for him to bring the girl. He watched his friend race off, then turned to hurry the girl along.

Only she wasn't there.

He spotted her ducking behind a pile of cardboard boxes and smirked. "Hidin' back there won't do you any good, Melanie. Come on out."

A metallic grating noise issued from the other side of the cartons.

"What the blazes!" Hickok exclaimed, and dashed past the boxes to discover an open door and a dark hallway. He stepped inside and glanced both ways. To his left he detected movement, so he started in pursuit, moving at a brisk walk, wary of blundering into a trap. He realized that Melanie must know this section of Dallas like the back of her hand, and he would be at a disadvantage unless he could force her into the open. Faintly to his ears came the sound of her footfalls.

What kind of building were they in? he wondered. A business establishment of some kind. The dim lighting enabled him to perceive the vague outline of the corridor walls, and that was all. He came to a junction, and far down the branch to his right a scarecrow form fled. He debated whether to continue or go aid his buddies. Since Blade had maintained they needed the girl to lead them to the Chosen and left him in charge of her, he jogged after the scarescrow.

The light became brighter the farther he went. In 40 yards the hallway veered sharply to the left, and he spied a partially open door 20 feet distant. En route to the exit he passed a number of other doors, all closed. His intuition told him Melanie wasn't hiding inside, and he sprinted to the exit and shoved the door open.

A wide, deserted street stretched to the north and the south. Directly across the street reared a squat, long structure, outside of which, littering the sidewalk and the asphalt, were 25 or 30 peculiar rusted carts lying on their sides or overturned with their four small wheels jutting into the air. Atop the building, its southern third missing, was a sign. Eight faded black letters were legible.

ERMARKET.

What the dickens was that?

Hickok moved to the middle of the street.

The front of the ERMARKET had once consisted of a series of glass panes, and busted pieces of glass dotted the ground. At the north corner a shattered glass door provided a means of entering. From within the structure there arose a loud crash, the clatter of objects falling, and then a muffled curse.

That girl must be the biggest klutz on the planet! Hickok thought, and went in pursuit of her. He walked into the run-down building warily. To his left was a row of counters, and on each one there rested a mechanical or electronic contrivance, a square affair bearing buttons imprinted with numbers and figures. Beyond the counters were 12 wide aisles.

Thanks to the sunlight streaming in the front of the store, Hickok could perceive details clearly. Trash covered the white tile floor in spots; torn cartons and packages and open tin cans were especially numerous. Flies swarmed above certain aisles. He crinkled his nose when he detected a subtle, putrid scent.

Despite the light, the place gave him the creeps.

Hickok stepped to the first aisle, noting the barren shelves and the litter. He decided the place had once been a thriving food store.

Something clicked way in the back.

Klutzy again? he wondered, and moved to the second aisle, then the third, going from one to the other. He paused at the head of the sixth aisle, intrigued by a pair of black doors located at the rear of the store. Proceeding quickly, he checked each of the remaining aisles and returned to the central one.

Where did those doors lead?

The Warrior strode down the aisle and leaned against the wall to the right of the black doors. To his surprise, he found that the twin doors were constructed of a leather or plastic substance instead of wood or metal. He gingerly reached out with his right hand and pressed on the nearest door, which swung inward several inches. In contrast to the store proper, the room or chamber on the far side was plunged in inky darkness.

Would Melanie hide back there?

The odd clicking sounded again.

Hickok knew the girl had to be aware he was on her heels, eliminating the need for extreme stealth. He chuckled and shoved the door all the way open. "Come out, come out, wherever you are!" he declared playfully.

No one responded.

"Come on, Melanie. I know you're in here," Hickok bluffed, hoping she would give up so he could speed to his friends.

Still no answer.

Hickok took a step into the rather dank chamber, trying to gauge its dimensions, and came to conclusion he was in an enormous area that might have been used to stock the items sold in the store. He glimpsed cartons scattered here and there. Four narrow windows, approximately 50 feet from the doors and 20 feet above the floor, afforded scant illumination.

From off to the left came more clicking.

"I won't hurt you, Melanie," Hickok promised. "Do us both a favor and come out here."

She didn't reply.

"Please."

Silence.

Exasperated, Hickok felt tempted to forget about her and head for the alley. But Blade had ordered him to bring her, and he'd bring her or die in the attempt. Knowing his companions were in danger, even though he possessed total confidence in their ability to take care of themselves, disturbed him immensely. Preoccupied with his worry, he released the door and advanced several yards into the cavernous chamber.

Feet scuttled across the floor to his right.

"Melanie?"

The loud clicking was repeated to the left.

And suddenly Hickok knew with an awful certainty that he wasn't alone. There were—things—all around him. He had made the cardinal mistake any Warrior could make: He'd been careless. If he wanted to live, and he sure as heck did, then he'd better move, and move fast. The thought brought instant action. He darted for the black doors.

But as swift as the gunman was, there were—things—that were much swifter.

Hickok heard the scuttling again, and what felt like an iron hand clamped on his right heel, tripping him, causing him to fall onto his hands and knees. He glanced over his left shoulder, his skin prickling as he distinguished the broad, inhuman shape of his attacker. Whatever it was, the creature stood four feet high and was equally as wide.

The grip on his heel tightened.

More scuttling noises arose from nearby.

Hickok twisted, snapped the Henry to his shoulder, and fired twice, the shots thundering and reverberating in the chamber. The first shot rocked the thing, the second drove it backwards, clicking furiously.

His ankle was free!

Rising awkwardly, his right heel lanced with pain, Hickok managed to take two strides and get within three feet of the doors before a heavy body plowed into him from the left, bowling him over. He tumbled and rolled, concentrating on keeping hold of the Carbine at all costs, and wound up flat on his back. Before he could push to his feet, another of the creatures materialized above his head. A snakelike arm or appendage slithered across his neck.

The thing clicked.

Hickok angled the Henry upward, levered in a fresh round, and squeezed the trigger, bracing the stock against his hip to absorb the recoil. The shot flipped the creature into the gloom. He scrambled up, spotted the doors, and took four steps.

A scuttling express train swept out of the darkness and rammed the gunman in the legs.

This time Hickok went down extremely hard, his jaw taking the brunt of the impact, his mouth snapping shut and his upper and lower teeth mashing together. A universe of stars burst into being in front of his eyes, his body went slack, and he couldn't seem to organize any coherent thoughts.

The same or a similar iron hand seized the gunman's right leg, and the next moment whatever held him was dragging him deeper into the chamber.

A chorus of clicking sounded.

Slowly, through the haze, his muddled mind became aware that the creature dragging him wasn't alone. Many others were serving as escorts. He was completely surrounded by a clicking pack of the things. With a start, he felt the Henry begin to slip from his grasp. His right hand closed on the shoulder strap, and he clutched the strap with all the strength he could muster, pulling the rifle after him.

Where were they taking him?

Hickok kept himself as limp as he could, certain the whole bunch would pounce on him if he were to put up a fight at this point. He allowed his mind to clear, gathering his wits, biding his time until a better opportunity to escape should arise. Although the pressure on his right leg where the thing held him was intense, making the leg throb in torment, he doubted the skin or any bones were broken. As long as he didn't panic, he might be able to get out of the fix he was in in one piece.

The clicking continued unabated.

Were they communicating? Hickok wondered. Were the creatures talking to one another, using those clicks instead of speech? He reasoned that his attackers must be some form of mutation.

But what?

A cool, damp breeze suddenly touched his face.

Thanks to the light from one of the narrow windows, Hickok was able to distinguish the outline of a huge hole in the back wall. He gulped when he realized the things were taking him into it, and he resisted an urge to try and flee. Seconds later the cement floor over which he had been drug was replaced by loose, moist earth. He could smell the dank soil, and he worried about dirt clogging the Henry. Surreptitiously, pulling the Carbine toward him inch by snail-paced inch, he succeeded in grasping the barrel and hugging the rifle to his chest.

The tunnel slanted downward for a half-dozen yards, then leveled.

Hickok lost track of the distance they traveled. Total blackness engulfed him. He began to doubt the wisdom of not trying to break loose sooner. If the creature let go of him now, he'd have no way of knowing which way led to safety. He'd blunder about in the darkness until starvation or a mutation claimed him.

Blast!

Here was another fine mess he'd gotten himself into.

He thought of Sherry, Ringo, and Chastity, and smiled. Even if he bought the farm, he'd try and go out thinking of them, the three people who loved him more than any others, the three who meant more to him than life itself. Funny, wasn't it, how life worked out sometimes? When he'd been much younger, he'd believed that no woman in her right mind would ever tie the knot with him. There had been a woman he cared for before he met Sherry, another Warrior named Joan, but after she was killed by the lousy Trolls he'd resigned himself to the prospect of possibly being a bachelor for life. And then along came the most wonderful female on the planet, someone who viewed him as special, someone who must have hit her head on a rock when she was a child.

Hickok almost laughed aloud.

Unexpectedly the passageway brightened, and moments later the clicking creatures and their captive emerged from the tunnel into another immense chamber. Regularly spaced windows set high on the four walls allowed the sunlight to reach the floor.

Hickok looked to his right, and his blood seemed to chill in his veins. Although the lighting wasn't sufficient to reveal every feature, he could see his captors better, and what he saw shocked him.

They were bugs.

Big, ugly bugs.

The insects were about the size of mule deer, but twice as wide. Their bodies were oval in shape, and each was supported by six thin legs. Every insect sported a pair of wings that rested flat on top of its streamlined bulk. From the head of each creature extended a pair of antennae over six feet in length, and the antennae were constantly in motion, swaying and waving or flicking out to touch other insects. Underneath each gruesome head, and used to produce the clicking noises, were a pair of mandibles.

Hickok could feel goose bumps all over his flesh. He glanced down at his legs, at the insect holding him in its steely mandibles, and he wished he could plug the vermin and skedaddle.

But not yet.

He estimated there were 15 of the bugs around him, and he knew he couldn't down them all before they got him. So he waited, hoping for a break.

The insects moved across the floor until they came to a strange mound almost ten feet in height. They climbed effortlessly up the gradual incline.

Hickok turned his head, studying the composition of the mound. To his amazement, he determined the bugs were ascending an artificial hill composed of trash, perhaps the accumulation of decades. The stench was nauseating.

The creatures attained the rim and paused.

Gazing down, Hickok could see that the interior of the mound resembled a miniature volcano. There was a nine-foot drop to a circular flat area that had been packed down or scooped out. The light from the windows only partly illuminated the flat area, but there was enough to disclose the grisly white objects cluttering the bottom.

Hickok's eyes widened.

For there, dotting the floor of the mound, lay a score of human skeletons.

CHAPTER ELEVEN

"The way I read it, the woman ran in here first and Hickok went in after her," Geronimo said.

"Then we go after him," Blade said, and motioned at the leader of the Chains. "Get over here."

Marlon warily stepped closer. "What?"

"Where would she go from here?" Blade asked.

"How should I know?" Marlon retorted.

"She's your fox, as you put it," Blade reminded him. "Where would she go with someone chasing her?"

"Anywhere," Marlon said. "We don't have special hiding places, if that's what you mean. Melanie knows this area really well. She'll probably lose your friend in no time flat."

Blade sighed. "Okay, Geronimo lead off," he said, then reached out, grabbed Marlon by the right shoulder, and shoved the young tough between Geronimo and himself. "You'll walk in front of me," he instructed. "Any funny moves and I'll split your skull. Understood?"

"Understood," Marlon acknowledged sullenly.

"Lieutenant Garber, bring up the rear. Stay alert," Blade ordered.

"Will do, sir," the officer replied.

Without another word they entered the building. On a hunch, Geronimo bore to the left and walked until he came to a junction. He paused, eyeing both branches. "Which way?"

"Pick one," Blade said.

Geronimo studied the two branches for several seconds and noticed the light seemed slightly brighter at the end of the right fork. "We go right," he declared, and suited his action to his words.

"Any chance of my getting my guns back?" Marlon asked as he followed the Indian."

"None," Blade said.

"I don't like being unarmed."

"Who does?"

"Particularly in here," Marlon went on. "There are all kinds of creepy-crawlies in these old buildings."

"We know," Blade said. "We ran into a bunch of lizards on our way in."

"The lizards are the least of our worries," Marlon commented without elaborating.

They hiked in silence to where the corridor turned abruptly to the left.

"There's an open door!" Geronimo declared, and hurried to the exit. Once outside, he stared at the sidewalk, the curb, and the asphalt covering the street, and frowned.

Marlon, Blade, and Garber came through the doorway.

"What's wrong?" the officer inquired, noting Geronimo's peeved expression.

"No tracks."

"What?" Garber asked.

Geronimo pointed at the sidewalk. "Concrete doesn't hold prints very well unless it's wet."

Lieutenant Garber gazed at the curb and the street. "Oh. Then we're stymied temporarily, aren't we? We can't track them. What do we do now?"

"It's up to Blade," Geronimo said.

"Perhaps we should stay put," Lieutenant Garber proposed. "Hickok might return to this spot."

Blade ran his left hand through his hair, pondering their next move. Garber had a point about the gunman returning. They shouldn't stray very far from the alley. He decided to return and await Hickok. As he rotated toward the doorway he noticed a sign on the building across the street. ERMARKET.

"Listen," Geronimo suddenly stated.

"I don't hear anything," Lieutenant Garber remarked.

Blade cocked his head, and to his ears came the sounds of laughter and indistinct cries.

"It's the Chosen!" Marlon exclaimed.

"How do you know?" Blade inquired.

"I know. Trust me," Marlon said, facing to the south, his fingers twitching nervously. "We've got to hide or they'll nail us."

"They're coming toward us," Geronimo announced.

"Back inside," Blade commanded, and hustled them into the hallway. He stepped in last, then eased the door almost shut, leaving a three-inch space through which he could watch the street.

"I've got to warn the Chains!" Marlon declared.

"You're not going anywhere," Blade said.

"At least give me my damn guns."

"Not yet."

Marlon uttered an oath under his breath.

In less than a minute the pounding of running feet became audible, and Blade beheld a solitary figure racing down the center of the street, a man attired in torn jeans and brown shoes. He was shirtless, and the sweat glistened on every pore of his chest and shoulders. Looped around his slim waist was a chain. Blade glanced at Marlon. "Is this guy one of your gang?"

"Who?" Marlon responded. He moved to the doorway and peered out. "Son of a bitch! That's Gary! Yeah, he's one of the Chains."

"What's he doing by himself?"

"I don't know. He disappeared about four days ago," Marlon divulged.

Other figures became visible, sprinting in pursuit of the man named Gary, 30 yards to his rear and narrowing the gap rapidly.

Blade's eyes narrowed.

Gary appeared to be on his last legs. His chest heaved and his legs pumped sluggishly. He looked over his right shoulder and nearly stumbled. "No!" he wailed.

There were 18 pursuers, and they were evidently making a game of the chase, laughing and shouting to one another. Ten of the 18 were men, and only they wore any clothing, loincloths covering their privates. All of the women were stark naked.

Blade felt a surge of excitement.

Green splotches dotted the skin of both the men and the women, irregular marks evincing no clear-cut pattern.

"The Chosen!" Marlon hissed.

Here was a golden opportunity to take a prisoner and complete the mission! Blade smiled and hefted the M60. A few of the Chosen were straggling well behind the rest. All he had to do was wait for the main pack to pass the door, then leap out and grab the last of the stragglers before the rest knew what happened. The simplicity of his plan delighted him.

Gary was now 15 yards south of the door, and he had slowed to a virtual walk. He appeared about to keel over from exhaustion.

Blade tensed and held his breath. Keep going! his mind shrieked. Don't stop now!

But Gary needed more than mental encouragement. He faltered and sagged to his knees, breathing raggedly, swaying from side to side, his countenance pale.

"Look at him!" one of the women after him shouted gleefully.

"He's ours!" yelled a skinny man.

Many of the Chosen laughed.

Marlon glanced at Blade. "We've got to help him."

"Forget it."

"He's one of the Chains," Marlon protested. "I can't let those bastards snatch him."

"There's nothing you can do. If you went out there, they'd

capture you too.''

"Not if I had my guns."

Blade scanned the Chosen, noting they were armed with a variety of weapons: rifles, handguns, knives, clubs, and more. "You still wouldn't stand a chance."

"I've got to try," Marlon said, and the next instant he flung the door wide and ran toward Gary.

"Damn!" Blade fumed, exposed in the doorway for the approaching Chosen to see.

"Gary!" Marlon bellowed.

The onrushing group of Chosen slowed, taken aback by the unexpected appearance of Marlon and the giant. One of their number, a tall man holding an iron bar, waved his weapon in the air excitedly. "Look! Two more!" The rest responded with whoops and hollers, and they charged.

Blade was in a quandary. The opportunity to grab a captive without a fight was ruined. He felt no compulsion to intervene to save the man called Gary. By all rights he should return to the alley and hold out there until Hickok returned. But he did feel obligated to Marlon because he'd confiscated the Taurus revolvers. If Marlon died now, then Blade knew he must shoulder a portion of the responsibility for disarming the Chains' leader.

Marlon reached Gary and leaned down to help the man rise.

"Get them!" barked one of the Chosen.

Blade estimated there were 19 yards between the two Chains and the Chosen. Marlon and Gary wouldn't be able to reach cover in time. "Damn!" he snapped again, and jogged to the left, to the curb, wanting the angle to be just right. He raised the M60 barrel and fired, and he saw the heavy rounds tear through the pack of Chosen like buckshot through a paper target. Seven of them dropped in half as many seconds.

The Chosen retaliated. A woman swung a rifle to her shoulder and snapped off a shot, and others followed her example.

Marlon had his right arm around Gary's shoulders and was bracing Gary as the man shuffled toward the curb.

Undaunted by the bullets striking the ground and the walls
to his rear, Blade mowed down four more of the Chosen. He
saw three stragglers turn and flee, leaving four to contend with.

Through the doorway came Geronimo and Lieutenant
Garber, shooting as they ran.

Gary abruptly stiffened and clutched at his back, then fell
forward.

Two of the four Chosen fell, and Blade, Geronimo, and
Garber concentrated their fire on the remaining pair. In
seconds the duo were dead.

Blade stared at the perforated bodies for a moment, at the
blood oozing from the holes, exasperated at the turn of events.
He glanced at the fleeing trio, who were now 30 yards distant
and hauling butt. A sob drew his attention to the two Chains.

Gary lay on the asphalt on his back, his head cradled in
Marlon's hands. He sobbed again, his features contorted in
agony. Crimson drops formed at the corners of his mouth.

Holding the M60 in the crook of his left elbow, Blade walked
over. "How is he?"

The leader of the Chains shook his head sadly.

"Marlon?" Gary said, his eyes open but unfocused.

"I'm here."

"Where?"

"Right here," Marlon assured him, taking Gary's hand.
"Right here, old friend."

"They jumped me when I was scrounging over by the
Plaza," Gary said, his voice weak.

"There's no need to talk," Marlon responded.

"Oh, God! I hurt!" Gary cried.

Marlon bowed his head.

"They made me drink it," Gary stated.

"Drink what?"

"The Elixir."

"The what?"

"The Elixir of Life. That's how they do it," Gary said.

"What do they do?" Marlon inquired.

Instead of replying, Gary blinked and inhaled deeply. "This

world sucks," he declared, and went limp.

"Gary?" Marlon said, shaking him gently. "Gary?"

"He's gone," Blade said.

"Gary was one of my best friends," Marlon said. "This is one more I owe these bastards for."

"What did he mean about the Elixir of Life?" Blade questioned.

"Beats me. I never heard about it before."

"Uh-oh!" Geronimo suddenly interjected, staring to the south.

Blade looked at his friend, then pivoted. Seventy yards off were the three stragglers. They had halted and were conversing with another large party of the Chosen, perhaps 30 or more. Had the second party been nearby, heard the shots, and came to investigate? The Chosen seemed to be all over the city. How many had Melanie said there were? One hundred and fifty?

"Here they come," Geronimo announced.

Sure enough, the second group of Chosen were advancing at a brisk clip.

Blade glanced at Lieutenant Garber. "Give Marlon his guns."

The officer hesitated.

"Now," Blade said, and faced to the north. If they retraced their steps to the alley, they'd undoubtedly be pursued by the Chosen. Even if they eluded the pack, the Chosen might linger in the area, posing a threat to Hickok when the gunman came back.

"Let's stand and fight," Marlon proposed, sliding his revolvers into their holsters.

"You can do whatever you want," Blade told him. "We're running."

"We're what?" Lieutenant Garber asked in disbelief.

"We're going to lead them off to the north, then lose them and circle around," Blade said.

"I'm not one of your men. I can do what I want," Marlon declared.

Blade jabbed his right forefinger at the second party. "Do

you want them to be nearby when Melanie and our friend show up?''

Marlon deliberated for several seconds, and finally shook his head. "No. I don't."

"Then stick with us and maybe we'll get out of this mess alive," Blade said. "You know the city better than we do. Lead the way. Find a spot where we can lose them."

"Fair enough," Marlon said, and jogged northward.

Blade ran on Marlon's heels. Pacing him on the right was Geronimo, on the left the officer.

"There's a place I know about a mile from here," Marlon stated. "A building that's a real maze. We should be able to lose them in there."

"Go for it," Blade said.

But they had covered only 500 yards when an unanticipated obstacle to their plan materialized directly in their path. Around the corner of an intersection 90 feet away appeared another pack of the Chosen.

CHAPTER TWELVE

The bug abruptly released him.

Headfirst, Hickok dropped toward the floor of the mound, toward the ghastly collection of human bones. He automatically whipped his legs downward, his marvelously coordinated physique responding superbly, and executed a flip in midair. His moccasins came down hard on the left thigh bone of a skeleton lying at the base of the circular wall of trash, and the bone snapped with a sharp retort. Hickok's momentum carried him to his hands and knees. He gripped the Henry firmly and stood, aiming at the rim.

All of the bugs were gone.

Hickok lowered the Carbine slowly, confounded. How in the world was he going to get out of this fix? he asked himself. The almost sheer face of the nine-foot wall would pose formidable difficulties if he attempted to scale it. If he could find something to prop against the wall for added support, he might be able to—

A crunching sound emanated from the shadowy half of the flat area.

Swiveling the rifle, Hickok's eyes narrowed as he tried to pierce the gloom. He assumed there must be a bug in there with him, and he waited for a hint of movement so he could blast away.

"Don't shoot! It's me!" cried a frightened female voice.

"Who the—?" Hickok blurted.

She emerged from the darkness, her hands clasped to her chest, her face a mask of fear.

"You!" Hickok exclaimed.

Melanie Stevens gave a nervous little wave with her right hand. "Hi there."

"How'd you get in here?" the gunman demanded.

"I thought I could lose you in the supermarket," Melanie said haltingly, her eyes roving to the rim. "I knew it better. I knew about the cockroaches—"

"The what?" Hickok asked, interrupting her.

"The things that caught us. They're called cockroaches."

"Cockroaches are usually dinky, pesky bugs," Hickok observed. "The radiation or the chemicals must've gotten to these."

"I was told they've been in Dallas since shortly after the war," Melanie said.

Hickok regarded her critically. "You knew the bugs were in that place?"

Melanie nodded.

"So you figured you'd sucker me in there and let the blamed cockroaches take care of me, huh?" Hickok deduced.

"Well, something like that," Melanie admitted sheepishly.

"What went wrong?"

"They don't like bright light, and I didn't think they would come out of the warehouse during the day. I hid at the back, near those black doors, and made some noise to get your attention. Before I knew it, one of the roaches pounced on me, knocking me over. My head hit the floor and I passed out. The next thing I knew, I was in this pit," Melanie detailed. "A few of them watched me for a minute or two, then took off. When I heard them coming, I hid. And here I am."

"Lucky me," Hickok muttered, scrutinizing the wall of trash.

"You don't sound very happy to see me."

"Where'd you ever get a cockamamie notion like that?"

Hickok responded stiffly. "I'm tickled pink at seein' you again. Next to havin' a rattlesnake in my britches, I can't think of anything I'd rather have happen than to bump into you again."

"You don't like me, do you?"

"Sure I do. You rank right up there with poison ivy."

Melanie frowned and fidgeted with her shirt. "I bet you're mad at me too."

"And who says you don't have any smarts?"

"You can't blame this on me!"

Hickok glanced at her. "Shucks, no. I wouldn't think of puttin' the blame on you. Personally, I reckon this is all part of a plot hatched by the Easter Bunny so he can take over the world."

"What?"

"Never mind. I doubt you're much into philosophy."

"What's philosophy?"

"The Elders at our Home practice it. Philosophy is the art of thinkin' in circles."

"Why would anyone want to think in circles?"

Hickok shrugged. "It beats thinkin' into a corner."

She stared at him in apparent confusion, then suddenly burst into tears. "You're making fun of me! You hate me!"

"I wouldn't say I *hate* you," Hickok said, frowning.

"Yes, you do!" Melanie insisted, and cried louder.

Hickok walked over to her and placed his right hand on her shoulder. "I didn't mean to upset you."

She covered her face with her hands and blubbered.

"We'd best keep the noise down," Hickock advised. "We wouldn't want to attract the bugs."

Melanie tried to stop crying, sniffling and whining softly. "I'm sorry," she apologized in a high, squeaky tone.

"We've got to skedaddle before those cockroaches decide it's supper time."

She lowered her hands and gaped at the scattered skeletons. "That's right. We're their next meal."

"Or their between-meals snack," Hickok said.

Melanie gazed at the top of the mound. "How can we get out? We're not tall enough to reach the edge."

"We can do it workin' together. Are you game?" Hickok asked.

"What choice do I have?"

The Warrior stepped to the wall and ran his hand over the side, marveling at how tightly the roaches had packed the material for their nest. He extended his right arm overhead. The rim was still approximately a foot and a half from the tips of his fingers.

"See? Even you can't reach it, and you must be six feet tall," Melanie commented.

"I can reach it with your help."

"What do you want me to do?" she inquired.

Hickok slung the Henry over his right shoulder and motioned for her to move closer. "Stand with your back to the wall," he instructed her. "Cup your hands at your waist."

She complied. "Now what?"

Taking two strides backwards, Hickok stared at the rim and tensed his leg muscles. "I aim to plant my right foot on your hands and jump. The strain will be terrific, but you've got to bear it or I'll fall on top of you. Savvy?"

"What?"

"Do you understand?"

"Oh. Sure. Why do you talk so weird sometimes?"

"How do you know it isn't everybody else who talks weird and I'm the only one who palavers normal?"

"Huh?"

"Never mind. We don't want to get on the subject of philosophy again."

"What?"

Hickok took a deep breath. "Are you ready?"

She gulped and nodded. "As ready as I'll ever be."

The Warrior swept into action, reaching her before she could so much as blink, his right foot coming down on her interlaced fingers even as he vaulted upward. He felt her hands start to give and flung his arms out.

Melanie grunted from the effort.

For a millisecond Hickok thought he wouldn't succeed, until his fingers closed on the rim and he dug his fingers into the compacted trash and held fast, dangling from the lip. He gritted his teeth and managed to secure a firmer purchase. So far, so good.

"Hey, you're not climbing out and leaving me, are you?" Melanie asked.

"Don't give me any ideas," Hickok told her.

"How do I get out?"

"We'll get to you in a minute. Keep quiet while I'll take a gander."

"A what?"

"Shut your face."

"Oh. Sure. Fine. Whatever you say."

Hickok started to pull himself up to the rim. Why, he wondered, was it always him who ran into certified cow chips when the Warriors went on a run? He seemed to draw them like a magnet drew metal. Once, just once, he'd like to bump into a genuine genius. At least an egghead wouldn't give him half the grief the idiots did. He inched his head above the lip and peeked at the mound and the chamber.

No bugs were in evidence.

Thank the Spirit!

"Okay," Hickok said, lowering himself again. "Start climbin'."

"You mean climb over you?"

"No, climb the wall," Hickok responded sarcastically.

There was a pause.

"I don't think I can."

The gunman sighed and rested his forehead on the trash. He toyed with the notion of shooting her and putting her out of her misery, but why should he waste a perfectly good bullet? "Climb up over me. Move as quickly as you can, and try not to gouge me with your knees."

"You can hold the weight of both of us?" Melanie asked skeptically.

"There's only one way to find out. And I'd appreciate it if you'd get a move on before my arms get tired. Any time this year would be nice."

"Boy, are you a smart-ass," Melanie commented, and jumped as high as she could. She caught hold of the Warrior around the waist, locked her legs on his, and clung to him.

"Keep going!" Hickok prompted her gruffly.

Melanie clambered higher, clutching at the sturdy fabric of his buckskin shirt. Her left hand found a purchase on his left shoulder, and she was able to place her right hand on the top of his head, then lunge at the rim. Her fingers slipped and she sagged, perching precariously on his shoulders and upper torso.

His arms feeling as if they were about to be yanked from their sockets, Hickok closed his eyes and focused exclusively on retaining his grip. His arms quivered from the tremendous strain.

Melanie tried again, her left knee inadvertently digging into the gunman's back. Her right hand grasped the lip, and a moment later she had both her hands on the rim. "I did it!" she cried, elated.

"Let the bugs know, why don't you?" Hickok growled.

She raised herself onto her elbows, arched her back, and swung her legs up. Once flat on the rim, she rested, grinning and breathing deeply.

"You're on my hands, you ding-a-ling!" Hickok snapped.

"Oh. Sorry," Melanie said, and eased down the mound, lying with her head near the lip, to the gunfighter's left.

Hickok began to pull himself to the rim again, his arms and shoulders aching terribly. His whole body shook with the effort. Sweat had formed on his palms, and he felt his left hand slipping. If he fell back in, he might be trapped until the bugs returned! Desperation seized him when his left hand came loose and he started to drop.

Melanie's hands abruptly closed on his left wrist and she heaved with all her might.

Using the added impetus she supplied, Hickok hoisted

himself over the lip and rolled onto his back, filled with relief. "Thanks," he said softly. "I reckoned I might've been a goner."

"There you go again."

Hickok smiled and sat up, scanning their surroundings. He extracted an ammo box from his left front pocket and hastily reloaded the Henry.

"I think the roaches are gone," Melanie said.

"Let's hope so," Hickok responded, replacing the box. He rose and hefted the Carbine. "Ready when you are."

"I'm right behind you," Melanie said.

The Warrior advanced down the slope, treading carefully to prevent his feet from slipping out from under him. He gazed at the windows, gauging their height at 20 feet, too high to reach without a ladder.

"How will we get out of here?" Melanie asked. "If we go back into the tunnels, they're bound to catch us."

Hickok had to agree. "Let's look for another way out," he suggested.

They came to the bottom of the mound and moved cautiously to the right, examining the walls, checking the recesses and the shadows for sign of a door.

The Warrior realized his mouth was dry and his skin prickling. He expected a horde of cockroaches to pour out of the darkness at any moment. There were too many of the creatures for one man to hold them off indefinitely. He wished he had Blade's M60. At least he'd have a decent chance.

Faint clicking arose from the direction of the tunnel in the far wall.

Melanie grabbed the gunman's right arm. "They're coming back," she declared.

"Keep your voice down," Hickok said, and hurried around the mound to the side farthest from the tunnel. He crouched down at the base of the nest.

Melanie imitated his example. "They'll catch us!" she whispered, horrified.

"They're not takin' me alive," Hickok vowed.

"Oh, great!" Melanie said, and snorted. "*You* can go out in a blaze of glory, but I'd like to live."

"Who wouldn't?" Hickok responded.

The clicking grew louder.

Angry at being thwarted when they were on the verge of escaping, Hickok glanced over his right shoulder at the rear wall. He peered intently at a vague outline in the corner, puzzled, his mind taking fully ten seconds to recognize the outline as the shape of stairs.

And where there were stairs, there must be a door at the top!

Overjoyed at his discovery, Hickok was about to grab Melanie and make a break when she unexpectedly took hold of his left shoulder and nodded at the sound. Hickok looked up, his grip on the Henry tightening at the sight of seven or eight cockroaches milling about the top of the nest.

CHAPTER THIRTEEN

"We're cut off!" Marlon cried.

Blade halted and glanced to their rear. Thirty-five Chosen were coming on at a run, now less than 50 yards away. In front of them, at the intersection, were another 21. To their left loomed a ten-story structure, while to their right was an abandoned department store.

Both groups of the Chosen were shouting and waving their weapons in the air as they closed in.

"This way!" Blade declared, and ran to the double glass doors on the larger building. He wrenched the right-hand door open and darted in to a broad lobby. Broken furniture littered the dusty blue carpet. Straight across from the glass doors was a long counter. To the left of the counter were two open, useless elevators, and to the left of the elevators a closed wooden door on which the word STAIRWELL had been stenciled in black letters over a century ago.

The others entered on his heels.

"To the stairs," Blade ordered, and loped toward the wooden door.

Outside, the increasing volume of pounding feet and aroused exclamations attested to the proximity of the Chosen.

"You go up first," Blade directed as he came to the door, gesturing for them to proceed.

Marlon and Lieutenant Garber entered the stairwell.

"What about you?" Geronimo asked, pausing in the doorway.

"I'll buy you time to find a back exit," Blade said. "Go with them."

"I'm not leaving you," Geronimo stated.

"I'll be okay," Blade said, patting the M60. "I want you to circle to the alley and wait for Hickok. I'll rejoin you as soon as I can."

"We'll hold them off together," Geronimo suggested.

"There isn't time to argue," Blade responded. "One of us has a better chance of eluding them than if we stick together. Now go! If Hickok reaches the alley before we do, he may tangle with the Chains."

The thought of the gunman made Geronimo's lips compress. "All right," he said reluctantly. "I don't like the idea, but I'll go. Take care."

"You've got it."

Geronimo hastened up the stairs.

None too soon.

Blade saw a cluster of people appear beyond the glass entrance, and he ducked into the stairwell and closed the door. Had they seen him? He pressed his right ear to the panel and listened, hearing the drumming of many naked feet in the lobby and upraised voices.

"Where'd they go?"

"Are you sure they came in here?"

"I saw them, I tell you."

"Somebody check that stairwell!"

Blade smiled, faced forward, and tensed. A rush of air hit him as the door was abruptly pulled wide, and there stood a gawking member of the Chosen with a baseball bat in his right hand. "Hi," Blade said. "You must be a whiz at hide-and-seek."

The man started to shout a warning to his companions.

Blade pounced, smashing the stock of his M60 against the man's left temple and crumpling him on the spot. He pivoted, finding dozens of the Chosen in the lobby, and cut loose with the machine gun, catching most of them unawares. The M60 roared and bucked, slamming the Chosen to the floor in bloody heaps of convulsing forms. Eighteen died before the rest began firing back at the Warrior. An arrow flew past Blade's head, and he backpedaled into the stairwell and closed the door.

But he didn't run.

Blade waited, his right hand on the doorknob.

"Son of a bitch!" shouted a man in the lobby.

"After him! After him!" shouted another.

"The Lawgiver will want to see him!"

"Hurry!"

Blade felt the knob shake as someone took hold of it on the opposite side. He clenched the knob securely, his muscles bulging.

"I can't open the door!" cried the man.

"Is it locked?" queried a woman.

"I don't know! Help me!"

A grin creased Blade's mouth as he pointed the M60 at the door, released the knob, and fired into the panel at point-blank range, the rounds punching through the wood, stitching the door with holes, as the Chosen packed near the stairwell screamed and screeched in torment. Blade let up on the trigger, whirled, and sprinted up the stairs three at a stride until he reached the first landing. He crouched behind the railing, resolving to delay the Chosen as long as humanly possible. Geronimo and the others would need a few more minutes to get clear of the area.

Enraged declarations came from the lobby. Men and women were cursing. The dying and injured wailed and moaned.

Footsteps pounded on the stairs.

Blade angled the barrel downward, his eyes narrowing. A quartet of Chosen appeared, bounding toward him, and he let them have a withering burst that hurled them from the steps and sent them cartwheeling below.

More screams and curses added to the din.

The Warrior surveyed his immediate vicinity, discovering

that three corridors branched from the landing. One hall led
to the rear of the building. The second diverged to the north,
and the third forked toward the front street. He opted for the
first, racing down the corridor, hoping to locate an exit. In
35 yards he came to another stairwell and rushed down the
steps.

Bingo.

Blade chuckled when he spied an exit door hanging open
several inches. Geronimo had undoubtedly used this same exit,
he reasoned, and dashed into the sunlight.

A parking lot stretched for half a city block.

He blinked in the sunlight, scanning the lot, noting two
rusted automobiles. A shout drew his attention to the west end
and he did a double take.

Damn!

It couldn't be!

But it was. Eleven armed Chosen were rushing at him.

Glowering in anger, Blade spun to the right, heading due
north, knowing Geronimo, Marlon, and Garber had slipped
away to the south. He ran to the sidewalk and paused, looking
both ways, relieved to see the coast was clear. If he went to
the left, the Chosen coming across the parking lot would be
able to overtake him easily. If he went to the right, he would
pass through the intersection located near the glass doors at
the front of the ten-story structure.

There was really no choice.

Blade sped to the right, his boots smacking on the asphalt,
the M60 in his left hand, the ammo belts slapping against his
chest. He bounded into the intersection and glanced at the front
of the building, hoping the rest of the Chosen were inside.

No such luck.

Approximately a dozen of them were gathered just outside
the glass doors. A woman spotted the fleeing giant and shrieked
an alarm.

"There he goes!"

Blade ran faster. What a big mouth she had! He scrutinized
the street ahead for a likely hiding place, believing all of the

Chosen who were after him were behind him and all he had to do was outdistance them to escape. An erroneous assumption, as it turned out.

Into the next intersection galloped ten horses, and astride each mount was one of the Chosen. Four of the men held rifles which they aimed at the Warrior.

"Surrender!" the tallest of the men commanded.

Blade halted so quickly he almost tripped over his own feet. He spun and saw over 20 Chosen strung out across the street.

"I won't say it again!" declared the tall man on the horse. "Surrender! If you're thinking of putting up a fight, forget it. You wouldn't stand a prayer."

The man had a point. Blade wanted to kick himself. He might be able to down half of them before they got him, but at such close range they *would* nail him, and throwing his life away senselessly was singularly unappealing.

"What will it be?" demanded the tall man.

Blade sighed and deposited the M60 on the ground.

"Bright move," the tall man remarked, studying the giant's face. "Don't feel so bad. No one has ever given us a battle like you just did."

"I'm just getting warmed up," Blade quipped.

The tall man chuckled and rode slowly forward, the other Chosen on horseback flanking him. "My name, by the way, is Aaron. How are you known?"

"Blade."

"That's it? No last name?"

The Warrior shook his head.

"Interesting," Aaron said, and reined in four yards off. "Where are your friends?"

"What friends?"

"Don't play games with us. There were three others with you," Aaron said.

Blade shrugged. "You must be hallucinating."

A woman on a white horse to the right of Aaron threw back her head, her dark tresses streaming over her shoulders, and laughed. "I like this one, Brother Aaron. He's witty."

Aaron lowered his rifle. "He's also dangerous, Sister Marta. Extremely dangerous."

"The Elixir of Life will tame him," Marta predicted.

"If the Lawgiver decides his soul is worthy," Aaron noted. Then he addressed the Warrior. "Kindly place your knives on the ground."

"I don't suppose you'd let me keep them if I promise to be a good boy?" Blade asked.

"Sorry," Aaron said, smiling. "The Lawgiver does not allow the impure to approach him armed."

"The impure?" Blade repeated.

"That's right," Marta chimed in. "Unless you are born pure or you're converted, you're not to be trusted. Sorry, lover."

Blade looked at the woman, who promptly winked at him and grinned. Perfect. Just what he needed.

"The knives, please," Aaron mentioned.

With the utmost reluctance, Blade placed the Bowies beside the M60. "Take good care of them," he said as he straightened. "I'll be taking them back soon."

Aaron chuckled. "Not unless the Lawgiver gives his permission."

"Who's the Lawgiver?"

"You'll meet him in due course," Aaron replied, and glanced at a woman on a black horse on his left. "Sister Ellice, I want him to ride behind you."

"No!" Marta interjected. "He can ride behind me."

Aaron shifted to stare at her. "How do I know you'll behave yourself?"

Marta made an X on her left breast. "Cross my heart and hope to die."

"I'm serious. You know you have a tendency to act up now and then," Aaron commented.

"Who doesn't, Brother Aaron?" Marta responded.

"All right," Aaron declared, focusing on Blade. "Climb on board behind Marta. Don't try to grab the reins and take off or we'll have to shoot you in the back."

"Can't I walk?"

"It's too far," Aaron said. "You'll have to ride."

"Don't you want to ride with me, handsome?" Marta asked in a miffed tone.

"I'd rather not ride with any of you," Blade said.

"Why not?" Aaron questioned.

Blade nodded at the tall man. "I like my skin the way it is." He braced himself, expecting an outburst of resentment at the reference to their affliction. To his surprise, Aaron and company laughed heartily.

"Your skin is safe for the moment," Aaron stated after a bit. "Climb on behind Marta."

The Warrior walked to the white stallion.

"Say hello to Victor," Marta said, stroking the animal. "He's the fastest horse in the city."

"How nice," Blade said politely. "Hello, Victor."

"Get on," Marta said, sliding forward several inches and extending her left hand.

Blade hesitated, his eyes roving over the green splotches dotting her hand and arm.

"I don't bite," Marta joked.

"It's not your teeth I'm worried about," Blade informed her.

She understood immediately and leaned down until her face was almost touching his. "I'll let you in on a secret, lover. Unless you drink the Elixir of Life, you won't get the Mark."

"Your condition isn't contagious?"

Marta laughed. "Don't I wish. Don't we all wish."

"Why?"

"It'd make everything a lot easier," Marta replied.

"We haven't got all day," Aaron remarked.

"Hop on," Marta directed the Warrior.

Relieved by her revelation, but wondering if she'd told the truth, Blade took hold of her hand and vaulted onto the stallion. The horse tossed its head and reacted skittishly to the additional weight.

"Whoa there," Victor," Marta said, tugging on the reins. "It's okay, big boy. Calm down."

The stallion obeyed, standing still and shaking its head from side to side.

Blade glanced down at Marta's naked back and buttocks, thankful Jenny couldn't see him now. He rested his hands on his hips.

"Hold on tight, handsome," Marta said over her right shoulder. "You can put your arms around my waist."

"I'm fine."

"Are you the bashful type?"

"The married type."

Marta giggled. "I won't molest you if you don't molest me."

"Fair enough."

"Unless you want to be molested."

"No thanks."

"Spoilsport."

Aaron motioned with his right arm, and the mounted Chosen moved straight ahead until they reached the line across the street.

"Brother Aaron," said a stocky man carrying a compound bow. A quiver full of arrows was attached to the leather cord used to support his loincloth and slanted across his left hip.

"Brother Ezekiel," Aaron said, acknowledging the greeting. "I'm taking the prisoner to the Lawgiver. Tend to the wounded. A detail will be sent to bring them back. Make a thorough sweep of this sector. If you don't find anyone else by an hour before nightfall, return to the Temple. We don't want you out when the mutants are abroad."

Ezekiel glared at the Warrior. "He took a terrible toll on our brothers and sisters."

"Gather his arms," Aaron directed, pointing at the M60 and Bowies.

"I hope he's judged unworthy and put to the test," Ezekiel declared bitterly.

"That decision rests with the Lawgiver," Aaron noted.

"I know. But I want to see him gored and trampled."

"Do you hate him, brother?"

"Don't you?" Ezekiel rejoined.

"I admit I resent what he did to our brothers and sisters, but think of the benefits if such a mighty fighter is converted," Aaron said.

Ezekiel considered the benefits for a moment, then turned his glowering gaze on Blade. "I'd still rather seem him gored."

CHAPTER FOURTEEN

Should they go for it?

Hickok estimated the distance to the stairs as 20 feet. Only ten feet separated them from the top of the nest and the roaches. The bug were bound to catch them if they tried to head for the hills. He decided to wait until the cockroaches departed, and he glanced at Melanie to insure she would stay put. She was scarcely breathing, her eyes riveted to the mound. He saw them widen and looked up, knowing and dreading what he would see.

A roach poised on the rim stared straight at them.

"Go!" Hickok bellowed, and shoved her toward the corner. "Up those stairs."

Perplexed, she stood and turned, taking a few precious moments to perceive the stairs in the shadows.

The roach on the rim started down.

Hickok gave her another, rougher, shove, and she took off like a frightened doe being pursued by a cougar. He raised the Henry to his right shoulder, aimed for the area between the eyes, and squeezed the trigger.

As it collapsed in its tracks, the mutation's antennae waved wildly, then fell flat.

Hickok retreated, risking a glance at Melanie and finding her only two thirds of the way to the stairs. He faced the mound in time to observe four cockroaches scuttling down the slope, and he levered off four shots in swift succession, going for the head in each instance.

All four went down, two onto their backs, kicking and thrashing.

Spinning, Hickok sped toward the stairs. He saw Melanie climbing rapidly, and he prayed the door at the top of those stairs wasn't locked.

Clicking sounded to his rear.

The gunman looked over his left shoulder, his skin crawling at the sight of cockroaches swarming over the rim. There were too many to count! He poured on the speed, his moccasins flying, his arms pumping. At the bottom of the stairs he stopped and whirled, sending a hasty round into the foremost bug and grinning when the impact flipped the mutation backwards into its fellows. He slung the Henry over his left arm and ascended.

"Move your ass!" Melanie bawled from above.

What did she think he was doing? Taking a Sunday stroll? Hickok halted on the tenth step, drawing the Pythons, and gazed down.

The roaches had reached the stairs.

"Hurry!" Melanie cried.

Hickok thumbed the hammer, working the double-action revolvers ambidextrously, firing six shots, and with each blast a cockroach stumbled and fell. He deliberately went for the leaders of the pack, and the six jumbled bodies formed a temporary obstacle for the bugs following.

"Damn your butt! Quit showing off and move!"

Showing off? Hickok dashed up the stairs and joined her on a narrow platform.

"I can't get this frigging door open!" she declared, nodding at a recessed gray metal door.

Hickok snatched at the vertical handle and lifted, using just two fingers on his right hand, but nothing happened.

"They're coming!" Melanie screamed, gazing down. "Get the damn door open!"

The Warrior slid the Colts into their holsters and grabbed the handle with both hands. He braced his feet and wrenched up with all of his strength. Still nothing.

"Oh, God! Please get it open!"

Hickok didn't bother to look. He knew the bugs were closing fast. Again he yanked on the handle, and yet again it refused to budge. The door must be locked after all!

Melanie gasped. "They'll be on us in seconds!"

Enraged at the prospect of being done in by a passel of mangy insects, Hickok absently, accidentally twisted the handle to the right, and the motion produced an audible snapping noise.

The door swung inward on creaking hinges.

Hickok seized Melanie's left wrist and forcibly propelled her through the doorway, then leaped through himself as something nipped at his left heel. He grasped the heavy metal door and heaved it shut, hearing the thump of cockroach bodies as they threw themselves at the door to get at him.

"You idiot! You almost got us killed!" Melanie said.

Taking a deep breath, Hickok leaned his back against the door and mopped at his sweating brow with the back of his right hand. "Is that a fact?"

"They almost had us!"

"No thanks to you," Hickok said, listening to the ruckus the bugs were making on the other side of the door.

"Me?" Melanie repeated in astonishment.

"Yep. You're the one who runs like a girl."

She sputtered and seemed about to fling herself at him. "What the hell is that supposed to mean? I *am* a girl!"

"I thought you were a lady," Hickok reminded her.

"Lady! Girl! Woman! What's the difference?"

"None. Most females run sort of funny."

Melanie's eyes narrowed. "We run funny? How do we run funny?"

"You know. Women sway sideways instead of runnin' straight."

A tremendously loud thud vibrated the metal door.

Her cheeks turning a beet red, Melanie clenched her fists and stepped close to the gunman. "If I was a man, I'd pound you to a pulp."

"Simmer down, for cryin' out loud."

"You swell-headed, stuck-up, stuffy, stupid son of a bitch!" Melanie exploded.

"Wow! Can you say that ten times real fast?" Hickok quipped, sidestepping her and studying the corridor in which they found themselves. Sunlight poured in a broken window five yards from the door, revealing a dusty, tiled hallway leading to a wooden door 40 feet away. "We'd better skedaddle before those varmints figure a way to get through the door or the wall."

Melanie glanced at the metal door, her anger dissipating in an instant. "Do you think they can?"

"I vote we don't stay and find out."

They hastened to the far door.

"Hold up," Hickok said, and took the time to reload his weapons. Once the Pythons were snug on his hips and the Henry was in his hands, he twisted the doorknob and eased the door inward.

An incredibly huge chamber stretched before them, bathed in the sunshine from large windows spaced at ten-foot intervals. Rows of enormous machinery, silent sentinels signifying the complexity of prewar civilization, were arranged from front to back. Dust caked everything, and a preternatural silence pervaded the air.

"Sort of spooky," Melanie remarked, gazing over the gunman's right shoulder. "What do you think this was?"

"A factory, I reckon," Hickok said, entering the chamber.

"It's too bright here for the roaches," Melanie stated. "We should be safe."

The Warrior glanced at the floor and halted, puzzled by a set of six-inch-wide tracks in the dust. "Maybe not."

"Why?" Melanie asked nervously, and then saw the tracks. "What made those?"

Hickon knelt on his left knee and inspected the prints. They were almost circular and there was no indication of toes or nails. "Beats me. I've never seen any like these."

"What if the thing that made them is still in here?" Melanie asked, scanning the machinery.

"It could be," Hickok admitted, standing. "Try not to wander off," he advised, advancing warily.

"I'm right behind you," she promised.

The gunfighter probed the spaces between the machines. Where could a critter hide, he wondered, when the gigantic gizmos, the benches, and the floor were all clearly illuminated? The tracks weaved among the machinery and were all over the place. Maybe, he hoped, the creature was nocturnal.

They covered 35 yards without incident.

"Look!" Melanie declared, pointing at a pair of doors visible far ahead. "A way out!"

"Keep the racket down," Hickok cautioned. "We're not out of the woods yet."

"Then let's get our butts in gear," Melanie said.

Hickok trekked another 30 yards. He paused next to a looming machine, staring at the dials and the gears, curious about its purpose. He'd studied books during his schooling years at the Home on various aspects of the industrialized societies dominating the globe prior to the Big Blast, and he knew there were once factories that manufactured everything from buttons to bombs, from toys to automobiles, but he had no idea what might have been constructed by the machines surrounding him.

A loud rustling noise interrupted his reflection.

"Did you hear that?" Melanie whispered.

"Yep."

"What was it?"

"How the heck should I know?"

"You're a big help."

Hickok stepped forward, mystified. Oddly, the rustling had sounded very near, yet nothing was in sight. The floor consisted of cement, eliminating an underground source. There was only one other direction from which the noise could have come.

Overhead.

The gunman looked up and froze, his skin crawling.

"What's the matter?" Melanie demanded, and bent her neck backwards. Her breath caught in her throat. "No!"

They were suspended in webs attached to the ceiling, from one end of the chamber to the other, patiently waiting for any prey to appear. Over a dozen bulky, squat, brown spiders fixed their mutiple eyes on the pair of humans. Each spider had a body as big as a full-grown German shepherd and thick, hairy legs. Each rested in its own web, the strands encompassing a 20-foot section of the ceiling. And the repulsive features of each were accented by two large fangs protruding from the center of a thin mouth.

"What do we do?" Melanie queried breathlessly.

"Well, it's a cinch we can't step on them," Hickok replied.

"Why haven't they attacked?"

"Maybe they're all takin' naps."

"Be serious!"

"Okay," Hickok said, placing his left hand on her back and shoving. "Run!"

They sprinted for the far doors.

Cocking the hammer on the Henry, Hickok ran on her heels, watching the spiders. If he survived, he planned to inform the Elders about the giant insects proliferating in Dallas. Giantism in insects and their close kin, arachnids, had become a common occurrence in postwar America. No one knew whether the giantism was a consequence of prolonged exposure to enhanced levels of radiation, or whether a genetic imbalance had been triggered by the chemical weapons employed during World War Three.

The spiders hadn't moved.

The Elders could ponder the issue of why there were so many giants in Dallas. Since the city had not sustained a nuclear strike, Hickok guessed the cause must be chemical in nature. He wasn't about to waste time puzzling over the matter in depth. Discovering the reason for mutations wasn't his bailiwick. Killing them was.

A spider suddenly plummeted from the ceiling and dangled directly in their path, ten feet above the floor, affixed to a thin, silvery strand. Its mouth opened and closed, its fangs dripping saliva or venom.

Melanie stopped and screamed.

Stepping to the left so the woman wasn't blocking his aim, Hickok sighted on the arachnid's eyes and fired. The thunderous shot knocked the spider from its strand, the slug tearing completely through its body, and the creature fell to the floor on its back, its legs kicking spasmodically.

The shot served as a signal for the remaining spiders to launch themselves at the floor.

"Go!" Hickok shouted, pushing Melanie, and she dashed forward.

Another spider materialized to their left, on top of a hulking machine, evidently intending to leap on them as they passed.

Hickok snapped off a round as he ran, and he was gratified to see the arachnid slammed backwards by the impact and disappear from view. He spotted another spider to the right, but it ducked behind a bench before he could shoot.

"There's one!" Melanie yelled, jabbing her left forefinger at a mutation hanging from a thread approximately 18 yards to the left.

The Warrior fired, the bullet unerringly on target.

Struck in the eyes, the arachnid swung wildly, its body spinning clockwise.

Three down.

Where were the rest?

Hickok scrutinized the chamber, hopeful the others were in hiding. He felt confident the Henry could keep those that appeared at bay.

"Look!" Melanie said, nodding at an object stretched across the aisle in front of them. She slowed, recognized the object as a skeleton, and jumped over the bones to continue her race for the double doors.

The gunman glanced down as he leaped over the dusty

framework of bones, noticing several busted ribs and two prominent punctures in the cranium. Near the outflung right hand lay an old sword. Whoever it was had gone down fighting.

They came within 40 feet of the doors, and still the spiders had not launched a concerted assault.

"We made it!" Melanie cried prematurely.

Hickok wasn't so sure. He wouldn't feel safe until they were outside the factory. With the cockroaches downstairs and the spiders upstairs, the plant served as a breeding ground for mutations. Possibly the cause was in the factory itself, either toxic chemicals or some other element the roaches and the arachnids were exposed to.

Melanie giggled as she rushed to the exit and placed her hands on the horizontal bar in the center of the right-hand door. She pressed on the bar but the door refused to open. "Help me!"

The Warrior reached the left-hand door and applied pressure on the sturdy bar with the same result.

"Kick it open," Melanie suggested.

Hickok took a pace backwards, about to enact her recommendation, when the nape of his neck suddenly tingled. He whirled, leveling the Carbine.

Less than 30 feet from the exit, forming a half circle and creeping toward the gunman and the woman, were 11 spiders.

CHAPTER FIFTEEN

"What about my weapons?"

"You heard me tell Brother Ezekiel to collect them."

"Yeah. But will he bring them to wherever you're taking me?" Blade inquired.

Aaron glanced at the giant on the horse beside his. "You seem rather attached to that machine gun and those knives."

"I'm fond of the knives," Blade conceded. "I've owned them for more years than I care to remember, and they've saved my life."

"They won't save you now."

Blade stared at the tall man. "So what about them?"

"Yes, Ezekiel will bring them to the Temple."

"Is the Temple your church?" Blade asked.

"The Lawgiver selected the site for our Temple of worship, for the center of our religious activities," Aaron said. "Legend has it that the stadium was used for a secular purpose before the war."

"Your Temple is a stadium?"

Aaron nodded. "You'll see for yourself shortly."

Blade lapsed into a moody silence, gazing idly at the sky-scrapers and other imposing structures as they rode to the southeast. The buildings in the central section of the metropolis were in better condition than those he'd seen in most major cities. He spied an immense sign on the roof of an edifice to the south and regarded it quizzically.

The sign depicted two men engaged in a peculiar form of combat or contest. Both wore strange uniforms imprinted with large numbers on their shirts or jerseys. Both wore bizarre spiked shoes. And both wore weird helmets covering their heads from their foreheads to their shoulders. On the front of each helmet, over the mouth of each man, was a handle for carrying the headpiece. The man on the left carried a bizarre oval ball tucked under his arm. In bold letters above both men were puzzling words: GO COWBOYS!

Blade racked his brain for an explanation of the sign. He knew about cowboys because Hickok was always reading books from the Family library on the Wild West. Cowboys wore Stetsons, sombreros, or other varieties of wide-brimmed hats, not helmets. And real cowboys had packed revolvers, not carried balls. He deduced the sign must relate to a type of sport, and he vaguely recalled skimming a book on American sports when he was much younger. It contained photographs of men in similar attire. What had the game been called? Tennis, wasn't it?

"There's the Temple," Aaron declared.

The Warrior shifted his gaze to the tremendous architectural marvel they were approaching. The sheer size and scope dwarfed the nearby buildings into insignificance. Curiously, there didn't appear to be any windows in the towering walls. The shape, from his vantage point, seemed to be circular.

"One day the Chosen will find the Temple," Aaron predicted.

"In a million years, maybe," Blade quipped.

"Much sooner than that," Aaron said cryptically.

"Not unless you breed like rabbits," Blade responded.

"I'm willing," Marta interjected, and snickered.

"One day the Chosen will fill the Temple," Aaron predicted.

"The Lawgiver wouldn't condemn me."

"Don't be so certain. He has overlooked your erratic behavior in the past because you were born pure. If you were a convert, he would have consigned you to face Destiny.''

Marta laughed lightly. ''I'm not worried, Brother Aaron. I'm one of the Lawgiver's favorites.''

''Don't say I didn't warn you,'' Aaron said testily, and kneed his mount ahead of Victor.

''The Lawgiver can have you killed because of your behavior?'' Blade asked.

''The Lawgiver has the power of life and death over the flock,'' Marta explained. ''If one of the Chosen should become tainted by the impure, then their name will be stricken from the scroll of glory.''

''You've lost me. Who are the impure?''

''You are one of the impure.''

''Me?''

''And everyone who doesn't have the Mark.''

Blade pondered her information for a moment, then looked at the green splotches on her back. ''Do you mean the green marks?''

''Yeah. The Mark of the Chosen.''

''Everyone who has the green marks is one of the Chosen?''

''Of course. And when the earth is cleansed, only the Chosen will remain,'' Marta said.

''Does the Lawgiver intend to cleanse the whole planet of the impure?''

Marta nodded. ''Starting with the Civilized Zone.''

''So the attacks on the sentry posts must tie in with the Lawgiver's grandiose plan,'' Blade commented.

Marta didn't respond.

''May I ask you a personal question?'' Blade queried.

''What?''

''Why do you run around without any clothes on?''

''The Lawgiver teaches us to be proud that we bear the Mark of the Chosen. If we wore clothing, we would cover the sign of our purity, and we should always display our purity before our Maker.''

''You're losing me again.''

She sighed and glanced back at him. ''Be patient. The Lawgiver will explain everything to you.''

"I can hardly wait," Blade muttered dryly.

They neared the stadium, crossing a wide boulevard and riding onto a vast parking lot. A half dozen of the Chosen emerged from doors at ground level and came toward the mounted party.

"Hello, Brother Aaron!" called out a muscular man carrying a Winchester.

"Greetings, Brother Judas," Aaron replied.

The two groups met in the middle of the parking lot, and the muscular man studied the Warrior.

"The Lawgiver will be pleased."

"I live to serve," Aaron said. "Where are you headed?"

"Out on patrol."

"Brother Ezekiel is in need of assistance in the northwest sector, at the Donogal Office Building."

"I know where it's at. We'll head right there," Judas said.

"May the Maker guide all your footsteps," Aaron stated.

Judas's group strode off.

Blade watched them depart as Marta urged Victor forward. "He mentioned the Maker. Was he referring to our spirit Maker?"

"None other."

"Are the Chosen religious?"

"What a stupid question. Of course."

"You're religious, and yet you traipse around without any clothes on," Blade remarked.

"The Maker created our skin. Why should we be ashamed of nudity? The Lawgiver says that nudity is purity, and purity is the Mark," Marta said.

"How convenient."

"You shouldn't make fun of the Lawgiver," Marta mentioned. "You'll live longer."

"Thanks for the tip," Blade said.

Aaron signaled for a halt when his party came within five yards of the doors. "Dismount."

"I'll stay and watch over the horses," Blade offered.

Grinning, Aaron shook his head. "Thanks just the same. Brother Micah will watch over our horses."

"Are you positive you can trust him?"

"Inside," Aaron instructed, nodding at the doors.

The Warrior obeyed, pausing within to survey a drab corridor. He felt a hard object jab him in the small of the back, and he gazed over his right shoulder to find the barrel of Aaron's Marlin .30-30 an inch from his spine.

"Just so you don't get any ideas," the tall man said.

"You don't trust me?" Blade asked, feigning a degree of hurt in his tone.

"As far as I can throw you," Aaron replied, and gestured to proceed.

Escorted by the nine Chosen, Blade followed the passage until they reached a junction. Aaron directed him to take the left branch, and a minute later they took a right at another fork. After they made five subsequent turns, Blade began to wonder if the tall man was deliberately trying to confuse him. Finally they went straight for 30 yards, along a wide corridor that inclined slightly upward, and stepped out into the sunlight. Blade blinked, adjusting his eyes, and when he stared at the scene before him, his brow knit in consternation.

"Welcome to the Temple," Aaron commented.

This was a temple?

Blade shook his head in amazement.

He stood at one end of a gargantuan stadium. Above and around him rose tier after tier of narrow wooden seats, an interminable number, ascending to the very heavens. The center of the stadium consisted of a green field approximately one hundred yards in length. At the near and far edges of this field reared a pair of outlandish metal uprights, with two tall vertical posts connected by a horizontal post. He tried to conceive of the purpose of the uprights, and speculated they might have been used in some sort of climbing contest.

"Keep walking," Aaron said.

Blade moved toward the field, scrutinizing the dozens of Chosen engaged in various activities, estimating over 80 men

and women were congregated on the field. To the north was
a group of about 20 listening to a husky man read from a book.
On the south side were a few dozen mingling and conversing.
In the middle of the field stood four rows of the Chosen, each
person holding a brown book at chest height. In front of them
stood an elderly man whose shoulder-length white hair and
flowing white beard set him apart from everyone else. The
elderly man wore a blue loincloth. His back was to the
Warrior.

What were they doing? Blade wondered.

The elderly man raised his right hand, and suddenly the men
and women in the four rows began singing a hymn, their voices
blending in practiced harmony.

Blade glanced at Aaron. "What—?"

"Our choir," Aaron responded with a smile.

"You have your own choir?" Blade repeated, stunned by
the unexpected discovery.

"Why are you so surprised? Did you think we're as barbaric
as the countless scavengers who continually pass through our
city?" Aaron queried.

"I had no idea," Blade said lamely.

Aaron snorted and gestured at the field. "Our beginnings
are humble, but eventually we shall establish a culture greater
than any this country has ever seen."

"How?"

"Ask the Lawgiver."

"Where is he?" Blade inquired.

"Allow me to introduce you," Aaron said, taking the lead,
crossing the field toward the choir.

For one of the few times in his life, Blade felt completely
baffled. The Chosen gave him the impression they were
genuinely religious, but how could their supposedly spiritual
nature be reconciled with the attacks on the sentry posts? And
what was the connection between their religious fervor and
the green splotches? Of even more critical importance was their
plan to cleanse the world of the impure. The Chosen were a
moral jigsaw puzzle with crucial pieces missing.

Aaron halted a few yards from the elderly man as the choir concluded the hymn. "Lawgiver, I ask your humble pardon for this intrusion."

The elderly man turned.

Blade couldn't stop himself from doing a double take. Like the rest of the Chosen, the Lawgiver's body was covered with the green splotches. Unlike the others, the elderly man's face was a shiny shade of green from his forehead to his chin. And what a face! The visage resembled a predatory bird of prey, an eagle or a hawk. A great, hooked nose divided a perpetually puckered pair of thin, cruel lips and a pair of eerie, dazzling green eyes. Wrinkles creased the Lawgiver's forehead and cheeks, suggesting an age well beyond the normal life expectancy.

"I've brought a prisoner," Aaron announced.

"So I see, Brother Aaron," the Lawgiver responded, his voice low and alluring.

"He put up quite a fight," Aaron reported.

"I can imagine," the Lawgiver said, raking the Warrior from head to toe with a penetrating gaze. "Goliath was undoubtedly of a similar stature, yet David slew him with a stone."

"We're conducting a search for this man's companions," Aaron elaborated. "They should be in custody by nightfall."

"Excellent," the Lawgiver remarked, and locked his uncanny eyes on the Warrior. "What is your name?"

"Blade."

"An unusual choice of names."

"I've always been fond of butter knives," Blade said. He saw the Lawgiver nod at Aaron, and before he could fathom its meaning, while his attention rested on the elderly leader of the Chosen, Aaron hauled off and rammed the butt of the Marlin into his abdomen. The exquisite pain doubled him over, and he clutched at his stomach.

"You must be taught to respect your spiritual betters," the Lawgiver stated in a condescending tone. "You will not speak unless I ask you a direct question, and any sarcasm will be dealt with severely. Is that understood?''

Blade nodded, straightening slowly, resisting an urge to knock Aaron senseless.

"I can't hear you, Blade," the Lawgiver.

"I understand," Blade declared resentfully.

"Good. Now let's proceed with the interrogation. Why are you in Dallas?''

The Warrior hesitated, debating whether to answer. If he kept quiet he'd undoubtedly receive a beating or be subjected to torture, and although he believed he could handle anything the Chosen dished out, the information was too inconsequential to entail making such a sacrifice. On the other hand, he might be able to elicit important intelligence if he went along with them. "Your people attacked two sentry posts on the border of the Civilized Zone," he said.

"And you were sent to investigate."

Blade nodded.

"Are you a soldier?" the Lawgiver inquired.

"No," Blade said, and knew he'd made a mistake when he saw a puzzled expression come over those unnatural green features.

"Why would a civilian be sent to investigate a military matter? Are you lying to me about your military status?''

"I'm a mercenary," Blade lied.

"But why would they send mercenaries? You see, I know there were five uniformed soldiers, plus yourself and two others, who entered our territory. You were kept under surveillance until you went too near the lair of the lizards. Why would they send mercenaries with their troops?''

Blade studied the leader of the Chosen, thinking fast. The man might be old, but his mind was as sharp as the proverbial razor. The Lawgiver had noticed an incongruous fact he deemed crucial, and he was determined to learn the truth. "They sent mercenaries because the brass couldn't get all the volunteers they wanted."

"Why not?"

"No one wanted to risk catching the plague."

The Lawgiver considered the answer for a moment, then nodded. "Yes, they would be afraid of the plague, wouldn't they?" he replied, and laughed.

Aaron and the others joined in the mirth.

Blade decided to take advantage of their temporary good humor and test how far he could push without retaliation. "May I ask you a question?" he ventured, putting an urgency in his tone.

Instantly the Lawgiver ceased laughing and his countenance hardened. "Didn't you hear me a minute ago?"

"Yes. But there's something I've got to know," Blade said hastily. "Will I break out in those green marks too? Will I wind up looking like you?" He tensed, hoping he sounded appropriately fearful, expecting another rifle butt in the gut.

Instead, the Lawgiver and his followers enjoyed another hearty laugh.

"I will, won't I?" Blade asked timidly.

"Whether you shall have the singular honor of bearing the Mark of the Chosen is in my hands," the Lawgiver said. "Your fate depends on your behavior." He paused. "I can understand your anxiety, and since I have a few hours until tonight's service, I will graciously answer all of your questions."

"Thank you," Blade responded, shamming a subservient attitude. "I have so many, I wouldn't know where to begin."

"I do," the Lawgiver said, glancing at Aaron. "Is my car ready?"

"Yes, Lawgiver."

"Fine. Then we will conduct our guest on a little tour."

"A tour?" Blade repeated.

"Yes. You have gone to so much trouble to uncover the truth of our existence. Ask and you shall receive, says Scripture. It is only fitting that we share our secrets before you meet your Destiny."

CHAPTER SIXTEEN

"Take cover!" Geronimo warned.

Lieutenant Garber, Marlon, and the 29 members of the Chains promptly hit the floor, sliding from their chairs and lying flat between the rows of auditorium seats.

From his post at one of the exits on the east side of the school building, which he had cracked open several inches earlier, Geronimo could see the street fronting the former elementary school. He watched as a patrol of six Chosen passed, going from south to north, apparently in a hurry. In a minute they were out of sight. "The coast is clear," he declared.

"I didn't think they'd be looking for us this far south," Marlon commented as he climbed into his chair in the front row. "We're over a mile from the Donogal Office Building."

"I doubt they were searching for us," Geronimo responded. "Maybe they were on their way to join the band who are doing the hunting."

Marlon gazed at the auditorium walls and the ceiling. "I don't like being cooped up like this. If the Chosen find us, we're trapped."

"We can escape before they surround us," Geronimo said.

"You hope," Marlon replied.

"My plan has worked so far," Geronimo mentioned.

"Yeah, but now we're a mile from the alley," Marlon

groused.

"You know as well as I do that the Chosen were conducting a door-to-door sweep in that area," Geronimo said. "If we had remained, then they definitely would have found us. As it is, you left two of your best men concealed near the alley. They have a better chance of avoiding detection than all of us would have, and they'll spot Hickok and Melanie when they return."

"If they return," Marlon said, amending the Warrior's statement. "They've been gone too long. They could be dead or captured, like your buddy Blade."

Geronimo frowned at the mention of his giant friend. From the roof of an apartment building near the alley, where they had gone after fleeing from the office building, he'd seen a mounted party of the Chosen riding to the southeast with Blade as their prisoner. His friend's capture had changed the entire focus of the mission. Taking one of the Chosen captive had become irrelevant. Geronimo's primary concern now was saving Blade and finding Hickok, and since, thanks to information supplied by Marlon, he had a good idea where the Chosen were taking Blade and no idea where to find the idiot with the pearl-handled revolvers, his first step was to rescue the head Warrior. Besides, the Chains would not be able to execute a search for the gunman until the Chosen had given up their sweep and left the area.

"I just hope you know what you're doing," Marlon said skeptically.

"It's time for the next step," Geronimo said.

"What's on your mind?"

"You found us a place to hole up for the time being," Geronimo remarked. "And we have men watching the alley. The next step is for you to send a message to the Stompers."

Marlon came off the chair with incredulity on his face. "What?" he exclaimed, and there was murmuring among the Chains.

"I want you to send a messenger to the leader of the Stompers," Geronimo proposed.

"You're out of your mind!" Marlon responded.

"Why?"

"If I send a man to the Stompers, they'll hang him by his heels, skin him alive, slit his throat, and then ask why he's there."

"Who is their leader?"

"A nasty son of a bitch by the name of Reeves. I hate his guts and he hates mine."

"And the two of you have never gotten together for a meeting?" Geronimo inquired.

"No. Never. Why the hell should we? Until the Chosen came along, the Chains and the Stompers were always at war. The Chains controlled all the turf north of Interstate Thirty, and the Stompers had the turf to the south. The only times we saw each other was when we were fighting. They'd raid our turf, and we'd strike back. Or we'd raid theirs, and they'd come after us. That's the way it was for years and years."

"Didn't you grow tired of all the killing?"

Marlon snorted. "No. It was fun, man."

"How did the Chosen manage to defeat both gangs and take over the city?" Geronimo asked.

"I've wondered about the same thing a million times," Marlon said morosely. "I mean, up until about four years ago the Chains and the Stompers were the kings of the city. There were around eighty Chains and seventy Stompers. We were pretty evenly matched. Then one day some of the Chains disappeared, and we figured the Stompers were to blame. Later we learned that some Stompers had vanished, and they figured we were responsible."

"But neither of you were," Geronimo deduced.

"Nope. It turns out the damn Chosen were grabbing members from both sides and converting them."

"How?"

"I wish to hell I knew," Marlon said. "One day a guy would be perfectly normal, then he'd disappear and a few days later he'd be spotted running with the Chosen, almost naked and covered with those green marks."

"Did that happen to all of the Chains who disappeared?"

"No. Some we never saw again. My guess is they were killed. Maybe they couldn't be converted. I don't know."

"How do the Chosen convert others?"

"It's a mystery to us. We've caught a few of the bastards and tried to make them talk. Even caught two of our own who had gone over. But none of them would spill the beans," Marlon detailed.

"So the Chosen grew stronger and stronger and now they rule Dallas," Geronimo commented thoughtfully. "How many Chosen are there?"

"There were about one hundred and fifty. But after the number your big buddy did on them, I don't know. It all depends on how many he wasted after we took off."

"And there are thirty-three Chains," Geronimo said. "How many Stompers are there?"

"I'm not sure. About twenty-five, maybe less."

"Which would give us about sixty, counting Lieutenant Garber and me."

Marlon's forehead furrowed in contemplation. "What have you got in mind?"

"I can't take on all of the Chosen by myself. If I'm to rescue Blade, I'll need help. By combining the two sides, we'd—"

"Combining!" Marlon blurted out, interrupting the Warrior. "Do you want the Chains and the Stompers to work together?"

"Yes."

Marlon tilted his head and chortled, and some of the listening Chains chimed in.

"Don't you like my idea?" Geronimo asked.

"Your idea is crazy! *You're* crazy if you think the Chains and the Stompers will join forces. We've been at each other's throats for too long to call a truce."

"You'd rather continue hating one another while the Chosen slowly but surely pick you to pieces?"

Marlon frowned.

"The Chains and the Stompers have as much at stake here

as I do,'' Geronimo stated. ''Maybe even more. I want to save
a friend, and you want to save yourselves and your city from
the Chosen. If the two sides had combined forces years ago,
the Chosen would've been defeated. But no. You let your
stupidity and your pride stand in the way, and the Chosen are
in control.''

''If you want to look at it that way,'' Marlon grumbled.

''What other way is there?'' Geronimo countered.

''He's right, and you know it,'' Lieutenant Garber interjected, addressing the leader of the Chains.

''Who asked you?'' Marlon snapped.

''Strategically, you don't have a hope unless the Chains and
the Stompers combine forces,'' Garber stressed.

Slumping sullenly into his seat, Marlon said nothing.

''Think of your children,'' Geronimo said.

The Chains all swung their startled expressions toward the
Warrior.

''How'd you know about our kids?'' Marlon demanded,
rising again and walking over.

''Elementary,'' Geronimo responded, and grinned at the
pun, wishing Hickok could be there to hear his witticism.
''People don't pop full grown out of the womb. Some of your
members might be drifters or scavengers you took into your
gang, but you must have children somewhere. How else have
have replenished your ranks over the years?''

Marlon placed his hands on his hips. ''Yeah. Some of us
have kids.''

''Melanie and you?''

''Yeah.''

''Were are they?''

''Hidden at the Galleria. Four of our women are watching
over them.''

''How many children are there?''

''Nine.''

''Then for the sake of your children, if for no other reason,
you should seriously consider my plan,'' Geronimo said. ''We
might be able to defeat the Chosen, to spare your children the

horror of being converted.''

''Not only that, but if you'll help us we'll put your case to my superiors,'' Lieutenant Garber offered. ''If they agree, and if you're cleared for immigration by our medical experts, all of you could move to the Civilized Zone. You could live in peace and security. You wouldn't have to live like animals anymore.''

Marlon gazed at his people. ''What do you think?''

''I like the idea,'' a man answered.

''It's for the children,'' said a woman.

''No more worrying about being killed,'' added a second man. ''It sounds too good to be true.''

Geronimo cradled the Browning in his left arm. ''What do you say?''

''Even if we agree, there's no guarantee the Stompers will go along with your plan,'' Marlon noted.

''We won't know until we talk to them.''

''But any messengers I send will be killed on sight,'' Marlon posed another objection. ''The Stompers will start shooting the moment they see any Chains on their turf.''

''Then send a messenger who doesn't belong to the Chains,'' Geronimo suggested.

''Like who?''

''Me.''

''Forget it.''

''Why not?'' Geronimo asked.

''Just because you're not a member of the Chains won't stop the Stompers from busting your head wide open,'' Marlon said.

''But I'd have a better chance than one of your own people,'' Geronimo noted.

''I'll go with you to cover your back,'' Lieutenant Garber declared.

''You're both wacko,'' Marlon opined.

''We don't have all day to debate the issue,'' Geronimo stated. ''The longer we delay, the more jeopardy Blade is in. Garber and I are going to find the Stompers, with or without your help. Which will it be?''

Marlon frowned, stared at the Chains, then slapped his right hand against his thigh in frustration. "Okay. I must be as crazy as you are, Indian. We'll take you to the Stompers. But remember I told you so when they blow your brains out.''

CHAPTER SEVENTEEN

"The spiders!" Melanie wailed, and screamed hysterically.

The instant his eyes alighted on the arachnids, Hickok's mind made lightning calculations. There weren't enough rounds left in the Henry to nail them all. Even employing the Pythons wouldn't insure he could stop the spiders from reaching them, not when they were trapped with their backs to the double doors. There was no room to maneuver, to flee. Which could easily be remedied.

"Save us!" Melanie cried as one of the gruesome abominations stalked toward them, only 25 feet away.

Hickok spun, pointing the barrel at the center of the double doors, at the circular metal lock at the edge of the right-hand door, and fired. The bullet struck the lock with a resounding whang. Without bothering to visually inspect his handiwork, Hickok took a stride and planted his right heel on the right-hand door. Both doors swung outward several inches but wouldn't open.

The spiders were closing in.

The Warrior braced his legs, then rammed the doors with his right shoulder, throwing his entire weight and power into the effort. There was a loud snap and the doors parted. He grabbed Melanie's right wrist and darted into a corridor, then handed her the rifle, placed his hands on the doors, and closed them. Expecting the arachnids to make a concerted rush, he planted his feet firmly and tensed for the impact of their bodies against the doors.

But nothing happened.

Perplexed, Hickok tried to peer through the narrow slit between the doors to no avail.

"Let's get out of here," Melanie recommended anxiously.

Hickok was reluctant to release the doors. He couldn't believe the spiders had given up. Maybe, he reasoned, the critters wouldn't stray far from their webs. Maybe they confined themselves to the factory proper.

"What are you waiting for?" Melanie goaded him.

The gunman glanced to the right and the left. To the right the corridor extended for 70 feet, passing a series of offices. To the left the corridor ran 30 feet to a glass door, surprisingly still intact. Visible beyond the door was a sidewalk and a stretch of blacktop. He nodded at the entrance. "When I let go, run like your britches are on fire."

"My what?"

"Run like heck."

"I'll beat you there," Melanie said.

"Ready. Set. Go!" Hickok declared, and relaxed his pressure on the doors. He turned to the left. Melanie was already a yard in front of him. Despite all the swaying, she could run with sure-footed swiftness. He followed, elated their escape would be so simple, glancing over his shoulder to verify the spiders hadn't come through the doors. Strange. He'd figured the arachnids would be a mite more persistent. They'd looked so menacing when he first saw them hanging in their webs on the ceiling.

The ceiling!

Hickok snapped his head up, his hands streaking to the Colts. The ceiling consisted of sheets of white fiberboard. Ten feet ahead a ragged, yawning hole had been torn out, and there, perched in the opening and ready to pounce, was a spider.

"Melanie!" he shouted. "Look out!"

She slowed and started to turn.

The Pythons flashed up and out, and Hickok squeezed both triggers simultaneously. The shots bored into the creature's head, tearing through two of its eight eyes, and the mutation recoiled, scrambling upwards.

Three feet from the hole, Melanie halted and gaped at the ceiling, her fear rooting her in place, the Henry clutched in her hands.

Hickok launched himself into motion, hurtling the intervening distance and leaping, his arms outspread, catching Melanie from the rear. His arms looped about her waist, his momentum carrying her forward. The passed under the hole and came down hard. Hickok released her and rolled to his knees.

Not a moment too soon.

The spider had dropped to the floor, missing them by a fraction as it descended, and now it came after them, its mouth opening and closing.

The gunfighter sent four quick rounds into the arachnid's head and it collapsed. "Out the door!" he barked, pushing erect.

Melanie, on her hands and knees, the rifle lying at her side, went to rise.

A second spider came through the hole in a prodigious bound, angling its repulsive form at Melanie. The mutation landed in front of its dead fellow and darted at its prey.

A terrified screech burst from Melanie's lips when the spider's mouth closed on her left leg, its fangs lancing into her flesh.

Hickok stepped to her aid. He glimpsed another spider suspended in the cavity, about to leap, and he swiveled and fired three times. The arachnid shuddered and retreated from view.

"Oh, God!" Melanie shrieked as she felt herself being pulled backwards.

The gunfighter reached her in a bound, holstering the Colts in a fluid motion and stooping to retrieve the Carbine by the barrel. He moved in close, swinging the Henry like a club, slamming the stock into the spider's eyes. Once. Twice. Three times, and finally the monstrosity let go of Melanie's leg and rotated, lunging at Hickok. He backpedaled frantically, reversing his grip on the Henry, and levered a fresh round into the chamber. Those glistening, dripping fangs were an inch from his legs when he squeezed the trigger, the rifle recoiling into his shoulder as the heavy slug tore through the arachnid and it stopped dead.

Melanie was holding her left leg and sobbing.

"Quit goofin' off," Hickok snapped, seizing her under the right arm and hauling her up.

"My leg!" she cried.

"Move!" Hickok commanded, supporting her as they made for the entrance. He heard a heavy body alight on the floor with a pronounced thump, but he didn't look back. In two seconds they were at the door. He gripped the knob and twisted, praying the door wasn't locked.

"They're almost on us!" Melanie yelled.

Hickok shoved and the door flew wide. He snatched Melanie's arm and propelled her through the doorway. Right on her heels, he bounded out and flung the door shut. She stumbled and went down on her knees, and he whirled to face the glass door.

A spider's hideous visage peered at them.

If the arachnids came through that door, they were done for. Hickok knew Melanie couldn't travel very fast with her injury, and he resolved to stick by her until the end. He waited, scarcely breathing, while the spider eyed them.

"Save yourself," Melanie said, lying on her back with her left leg clasped to her chest. "I can't run."

Hickok said nothing. He stared at the mutation, prepared to fire, every nerve on edge. A tense, awful minute elapsed. Suddenly the spider turned and shuffled off.

A sigh of profound relief escaped Melanie's lips.

The Warrior waited another minute, wanting to be sure, his gaze glued to the glass door. Except for the bodies of the two mutations he'd slain, the corridor was deserted. Satisfied the arachnids wouldn't venture outdoors, he stepped to Melanie and knelt by her side.

"Thanks for saving my life," she said sincerely.

"I didn't want you to give one of those varmints indigestion," Hickok remarked.

Melanie mustered a feeble grin.

"How's the leg?"

"It hurts like hell."

"Let me see," Hickok said, leaning over to inspect the wound. The spider had bitten her halfway between the knee and the ankle, its fangs penetrating her calf. Her brown pants had been torn, and there were two neat holes almost an inch in diameter in her flesh. Blood flowed from the bite and dripped down her leg. "Do you know what kind of spiders they were?"

"Big ones."

"No. Do you know if they're—" Hickok caught himself.

"Poisonous?" Melanie said, finishing for him.

"Yeah."

"Nope."

"Blast!" Hickok snapped. "Well, it's a cinch we can't stay here. We've got to find some water so I can clean the bites. And I'll have to cauterize those holes."

"Do what?"

"Poke a hot iron or stick into those bites," Hickok explained.

"Over my dead body," Melanie said.

"It's the only way to kill any infection."

"I'm in enough pain."

"Would you rather be dead?"

She pursed her mouth, holding her left ankle tightly, and shook her head.

"All right. Let's go," Hickok said, and slipped his right hand under her left arm.

"*You're not going anywhere!*"

The cold words, bellowed brusquely from close at hand, caused the Warrior and the woman to pivot to the north.

"Uh-oh," Melanie said softly.

There were three of them, all attired in shabby clothes, all leering triumphantly. The heaviest wore a torn black leather jacket and jeans, and in his hands, trained on Hickok, was a Mossberg Model 1500 bolt-action rifle. To his right walked a thin man who sported a Mohawk and carried a Ruger Number Three Carbine. On the other side was a short man armed with a crossbow, a quiver on his back.

"Friends of yours?" Hickok asked.

"No way. They're Stompers."

The trio halted ten feet away, and the man in the leather jacket chuckled as he took a bead on the gunman's forehead. "Shut your faces, turkeys! And drop the hardware!"

With his right hand supporting Melanie and his left holding the Henry by the blued barrel, Hickok knew there was no way he could clear his holsters before they fired. He frowned and slowly lowered the Carbine to the sidewalk.

"Now the fancy handguns," Leather Jacket said.

Hickok slid his right hand from under Melanie's arm and reached for the Pythons.

"Not so fast, friend!" Leather Jacket snapped. "Take your time. Use your thumb and one finger."

The Warrior complied, setting the Colts gently on the concrete.

"Good," declared Leather Jacket, relaxing and allowing the Mossberg to drop to his waist. He studied Melanie. "You're one of the Chains, ain't you?"

"Say no," Hickok whispered.

"Damn straight!" Melanie stated proudly.

"I thought so," Leather Jacket said., "I've seen you hanging out with them when I've been spying." He glanced at her waist. "Where's your chain? I thought all the Chains wore them."

"Not all the women do," Melanie answered. "I don't like to wear one because it gouges my hips when I bend over."

"And what nice hips you've got," Leather Jacket observed lecherously.

Standing on her right foot with her left suspended off the ground, Melanie wobbled slightly and touched her right palm to her forehead.

"What's the matter with you?" demanded Leather Jacket.

"Can't you see she's hurt?" Hickok snapped. "She was bit by a spider."

"Will she kick?"

"Once the leg is healed, she'll kick like a horse," Hickok said.

"I meant will she die?"

"She could. We've got to clean and cauterize the leg," Hickok answered urgently.

"Nope."

The gunman glared at the three Stompers. "What?"

"She ain't going nowhere," Leather Jacket said. "We couldn't care less if she lives or not. All we care about is having our fun before she kicks."

Hickok's eyes became flinty. "You'll stand around and do nothin' while a lady dies?"

"Oh, we'll do something," Leather Jacket responded, and thrust his hips forward several times. His companions laughed.

The Warrior clenched his fists, his nostrils flaring. He could feel the C.O.P. .357 Magnum riding snugly in its special holster on his left wrist. A distraction was needed, anything to divert their attention so he could draw the derringer. The small gun, only five and a half inches in length and slightly over four inches in height, packed a tremendous wallop. He'd loaded all four chambers with 158-grain cartridges; one shot would knock a man off his feet.

"First we'll off you," Leather Jacket said, smirking at the gunfighter. "Any last words?"

"Yeah. Have you always been so ugly, or did a cow sit on your face when you were born?"

Leather Jacket's mouth twitched and his eyes narrowed. "Mister, you just made a big mistake."

"What else is new?"

"I figured I'd waste you quick and painless, but now I'm

going to make you suffer,'' Leather Jacket vowed.

"How? Are you aimin' to gab me to death?'' Hickok quipped.

Before another word could be spoken, Melanie unexpectedly closed her eyes, groaned, and pitched forward.

The Warrior instinctively caught her, his arms encircling her bosom as she fell, and he let her down to the sidewalk gently, depositing her on her stomach. His forearms were momentarily concealed under her body, and he reached beneath his left sleeve and grasped the C.O.P.

"Turn her over while you're at it,'' Leather Jacket suggested. "Save us the trouble.''

The three Stompers snickered.

"I've got a better idea,'' Hickok said.

"Oh? What?'' Leather Jacket inquired sarcastically.

"Why don't I do the world a favor and plug you cow chips?'' Hickok asked sweetly, and grinned from ear to ear.

Sensing something was gravely amiss, Leather Jacket started to bring the Mossberg up.

Hickok's hands swept out from under Melanie, his right arm coming up, the C.O.P. gleaming in the sunshine. His first shot caught Leather Jacket squarely in the center of the forehead and flipped the man backwards. In the space of a heartbeat his second shot boomed, and the man carrying the Ruger took a slug in the left eye. The round snapped the man's head to the left, and he tottered sideways and toppled over.

The last of the trio, the man holding the crossbow, shocked by the abrupt demise of his comrades, tried to throw himself to the left as the gunfighter rotated in his direction. He stumbled in his haste, and his finger closed on the crossbow trigger.

But Hickok was still in the act of pivoting, and only his right side was exposed to the bowman. That fact saved his life. His keen eyes saw the bowman's finger tighten, and he lunged to the right to avoid the shaft. As if in slow motion, he watched the crossbow bolt speed at him and felt a slight tugging sensation as the bolt creased the front of his buckskin shirt and kept going. He also felt his heels catch on Melanie's prone form, and before he could prevent it, he fell over, landing hard on his shoulder blades. He angled his right arm upward, intending to snap a shot at the third Stomper.

The bowman had whipped another shaft from his quiver and was trying to reload the bow, stooping over to extend the stirrup and placing his left foot on the metal brace so he could pull the string back.

Melanie came off the ground in a rush, her right arm flicking out, swinging a two-foot length of slim, silver chain. The chain arced out and wrapped around the bowman's neck. He released the crossbow and clutched at the chain, and Melanie heaved with all of her might, causing him to lose his balance and fall onto his left knee.

Enraged, the bowman yanked on the chain and attempted to regain his footing. At the sound of a single shot his right eye dissolved and the rear of his cranium exploded outwards. His mouth wide in stark astonishment, he pitched onto his face.

"Thanks," Melanie said, "but I could've taken the jerk." She limped to the bowman and began unwrapping her chain.

"Where the blazes did you get that thing?" Hickok asked as he stood.

Melanie glanced at him and smirked. "It was wrapped around my tummy, under my shirt."

"But you told them you didn't have one."

"I lied."

The gunfighter chuckled. "You're one tricky lady."

She removed her chain and straightened, grimacing with the effort. Her left hand gripped her thigh.

"Is your leg worse?"

Melanie nodded. "It's throbbing from all the commotion."

"Then we'd best tend to those bites," Hickok said, moving to retrieve his weapons. "We were lucky you passed out when you did."

"Luck had nothing to do with it, dummy. I faked fainting to give you a chance to grab your little gun."

Hickok paused in the act of reaching for the Henry and

looked at her. "You faked it?"

"Yep."

"You knew I was packin' the derringer?"

"Of course, silly."

"How?"

"I felt it under your sleeve when I was climbing over you at the cockroach nest," Melanie explained.

Hickok's estimation of her rose even higher. "Well, I'll be darned." He proceeded to reload the rifle and his Colts.

"You'd better hurry," Melanie urged. "I really am feeling dizzy now."

"You'll be fit as a fiddle in no time," Hickok said, encouraging her. He hoped that the spiders didn't inject poison into their victims. If she had poison in her system, her fate was sealed. He slung the Henry over his right arm.

"Hickok?" she said.

"I'm hurryin'," the Warrior responded. "We don't want to be caught unprepared if more Stompers or critters show up." He quickly finished replacing the spent cartridges in his Pythons and slid the revolvers into their holsters.

"Hickok?" Melanie repeated weakly.

"I'm ready," Hickok announced, looking up just as she swooned. He reached her in one bound and managed to get his left arm under her legs and his right about her shoulders. She sagged against his chest, her eyes closed, breathing unevenly, and the chain clattered to the blacktop.

Blast!

Hickok scanned their surroundings, discovering they were on the west side of a parking lot, probably the parking area once used by the factory workers. He spied a shoulder-high hedge to the east, and stiffened.

Pressing through the hedge were dozens of armed men and women.

CHAPTER EIGHTEEN

"What do you think of my royal chariot?"

"You're kidding, right?"

The Lawgiver sighed and gazed at the scenery on his side of the car. "The heathen are pathetically ignorant."

Blade pursed his lips and pondered his predicament. Should he make a break now or later? He shifted and looked at the occupants of the rear seat. The Lawgiver sat on the driver's side, his white hair and beard whipping in the wind. In the middle sat Aaron, and on Aaron's right another of the Chosen. Both men held their rifles steadily, the barrels trained on the Warrior.

"This is the only functional car in all of Dallas," the Lawgiver commented.

"I believe it," Blade said. He'd been mildly surprised when they'd emerged from the stadium to behold a battered, rust-rimmed, faded green convertible awaiting them.

"One of my followers found the vehicle under an overpass south of the city," the Lawgiver elaborated. "There are plenty of old underground tanks to siphon the fuel from."

"What about the battery? It had to be dead," Blade noted.

"Do you realize how many abandoned warehouses there are in a city this size? And not all of them have been looted. We have a hoard of firearms, kerosene, lanterns, batteries, you name it. We also possess several generators for recharging our batteries.''

''Did you find any medicine?''

''Medicine?''

''Yeah. Bandages, splints, pills, cures for insanity,'' Blade quipped, and immediately felt a sharp pain in his ribs. He looked down at the Llama semiautomatic poking him in the side, then stared at the stocky man beside him. ''I hope your popgun doesn't have a hair trigger.''

''Don't insult the Lawgiver,'' the man stated harshly.

''That's quite all right, Brother Solomon,'' the Lawgiver said. ''We should expect such conduct from those who are impure.''

''Yes, Lawgiver,'' said the stocky one.

The sixth man in the convertible, the young driver, glanced in the rearview mirror. ''Lawgiver, how long will it be before all the impure see the light?''

''Be patient, Brother Uriah. In the fullness of time the Maker will convert the entire world.''

''Then it's true?'' Blade interjected. ''You intend to conquer the whole *world*?''

''Not conquer, convert,'' the Lawgiver said, correcting the Warrior. ''Eventually, only those who bear the Mark of the Chosen will exist on this planet.''

''No way,'' Blade said.

''Where the Maker's will is concerned, there is always a way,'' the Lawgiver responded. ''As the Maker's chosen servant, I will realize the divine will.''

''When did you first notice that you suffer from delusions of grandeur?'' Blade cracked.

''Your kind is so predictable,'' the Lawgiver stated. ''When logic fails, you resort to insults.''

''What logic?'' Blade retorted. ''All I've heard are ravings about dominating the world. Be serious.''

''I *am* serious,'' the Lawgiver replied. ''I'll try to explain sufficiently so you can understand. Over seven decades ago I came into this evil world, and I was the very first to be born bearing the Mark. For years I believed I was inferior because of the green spots on my skin. Not until I became a teenager did the full truth dawn.''

"What truth?" Blade inquired, raising his voice to insure he would be heard. He gazed at the speedometer, which turned out to be broken, and estimated they were traveling to the southeast at 50 miles an hour.

"My parents taught me to read at an early age, and one of the few books we owned was the Bible. I spent every free minute reading that precious book, and one day I found the passage that would give meaning to my life," the Lawgiver said. "Until that day I was an outcast, shunned by everyone but my mother, father, and sister."

"Your sister?" Blade interrupted.

The Lawgiver's expression became sad. "Yes, my dearest Esther, long since departed. She was born two years after me, and like me, she bore the Mark." He paused, frowning, then resumed his tale. "One day I read in Genesis about Cain and Abel. Are you familiar with the Scripture?"

"Cain killed Abel and was sent into exile."

"That's only part of the story. Before the Maker sent Cain into exile, the Maker put a mark on Cain so that anyone who met him would know he was under the Maker's protection," the Lawgiver said, and quoted from memory. " 'And the Lord set a mark upon Cain, lest any finding him should kill him.' "

"What does this have to do with your plan to convert the world?" Blade inquired.

"Let me finish," the Lawgiver snapped, and frowned. "When I was reading that story, the idea first occurred to me that there might be a divine purpose behind my own marks. I searched the Scriptures and found other references." He paused, recalling the passages. " 'He hath set his bow, and set me as a mark for the arrow.' "

Blade studied the Lawgiver's features, detecting a peculiar, far-off aspect to the elderly man's eyes.

"And haven't you read in Ezekiel about the mark the Maker put on his chosen, and how those with the mark were spared?"

the Lawgiver went on. "There are many more I could quote. One of my favorites is from Galatians. 'I bear in my body the marks of the Lord Jesus.' "

"I think you're misinterpreting—" Blade began.

"I knew then and there that my curse was really a blessing," the Lawgiver said, cutting the Warrior off. A gleam came into his eyes and he smiled serenely. "Instead of being afflicted, I was truly blessed. The Maker had selected me to establish the kingdom of heaven on earth. All the proof I needed, all the clues to the special relationsip I enjoyed with our Maker were right there in Scripture for anyone to read." He chuckled, and quoted more passages. " 'I have made a convenant with my chosen. Even him whom he hath chosen will he cause to come near to him. I have exalted one chosen out of the people.''

An uneasy feeling gnawed at Blade's mind. He knew, from past experience, that those who were affected by madness were totally unpredictable and supremely dangerous, and he saw in the transported countenance of the Lawgiver every indication that the man was pathologically demented.

" Where is God my Maker, who giveth songs in the night?' " the Lawgiver asked. "What does Psalm Sixty say? Oh, yes. 'Thou hast made us to drink the wine of astonishment.' " He giggled inanely.

"So you decided those green splotches meant you had a spiritual purpose to fulfill?" Blade asked, hoping to prompt the Lawgiver into continuing the narrative.

"There was no room for doubt. I bore the Mark of the Chosen, and since we were instructed to be fruitful and multiply, I did exactly that. Esther and I had nine children, and all nine were exactly like us."

"You took your sister as your wife?"

"There was no one else to take," the Lawgiver said. "It took me over a year to convince her of the righteousness of my cause, but eventually she came around. We went off by ourselves and hid in the woods, and while we were there I found the secret." He rubbed his palms together gleefully.

"What secret?"

"You'll see shortly," the Lawgiver said, and lapsed into silence.

Blade faced forward and placed his hands on the dash. Several questions had been answered, but pieces of the puzzle remained. He now knew that the Chosens' religious beliefs stemmed from the Lawgiver's interpretation of key passages in the Bible, an interpretation warped by the vindictiveness of a man who couldn't tolerate being born "different," a man branded by more than the green splotches on his body, a man who had to justify his existence by inventing a special link to Deity. He also knew the core of the Chosen were composed of the Lawgiver's own family. But the knowledge didn't explain how the Lawgiver was able to convert those who weren't born with the marks. And the knowledge didn't explain how the Lawgiver could maintain his sway over those who were converted. It wasn't as if the Chosen were zombies.

They drove to the south for seven more miles, encountering fewer and fewer structures the farther they went. Finally the convertible climbed a hill, and the driver braked and pulled over to a weed-choked curb on the left.

Blade surveyed the landscape. On the right was a sloping field. On the left, next to the curb, stood a sign partly destroyed by the passage of time and the ravages of the elements. It bore the words CHEMITEX, INC.

"Get out," Aaron ordered.

The Warrior climbed from the convertible, and the guards fanned out, encircling him.

"Come with me," the Lawgiver said, beckoning with his right arm.

Blade moved toward the curb, the guards parting to permit him to walk alongside their leader. As they walked, four large structures materialized below the crest of the hill. All were enclosed within a chain-link fence. A narrow path ran from the curb down to the fence, a distance of approximately 50 yards.

"My home," the Lawgiver said, nodding at the complex.

"You live here?" Blade asked in surprise.

"I did when I was younger. My family lived here for over thirty years."

"But why live at a chemical compound on the outskirts of the city when there are nice homes in Dallas for the taking?"

"My parents settled here a year before I was born for a variety of reasons. First, it's relatively isolated, on the outskirts as you pointed out, and the gangs, the Chains and the Stompers, seldom venture out this far. Second, the scavengers and the looters rarely bother with industrial facilities because there's not much worth taking. Third, it's not *too* far out. My parents could sneak into the city and hunt for supplies."

"Your folks lived here like hunted animals?"

"It's not that bad," the Lawgiver said. "See for yourself." He headed down the path.

Blade followed, scrutinizing the complex. The path led to a split in the chain-link fence. Three of the buildings at the site were rectangular in shape, while the fourth was square. On the opposite side of the CHEMITEX plant, in the center of the fence, stood a closed metal gate. Beyond the gate an asphalt access road meandered for seven hundred yards before connecting with a street. "Why didn't we drive in the front gate?" he asked. "Why go in the back way?"

"It's a security precaution," answered Aaron, who walked behind the Warrior. "We don't want to draw attention to the facility, which we would if we drove up to the front gate. And from the top of the hill we can see for miles. If anyone tailed us, we'd see them."

"I take it you come here often," Blade commented.

"Quite often," Aaron confirmed.

"But why, when you've taken over that stadium as your headquarters, as your Temple?"

"The Bowl serves as our temple of worship and for other activities," Aaron said, "but we can't obtain the Elixir of Life there."

"Why do you call the stadium the Bowl?"

"Legend has it that that's what the place was called before

the war," Aaron divulged. "The Cabbage Bowl, I believe."

"Enough conversation, Brother Aaron," the Lawgiver said sternly.

They descended slowly. Blade studied the layout of CHEMITEX, speculating on the purpose the complex had once served. Had the plant manufactured chemicals? If so, what kind? Warfare toxins, or chemicals utilized in agriculture or commercial industry? And how could a chemical concern be connected to the Chosens' Elixir of Life? For that matter, what *was* the Elixir? Perhaps the substance had something to do with longevity. "Do you take the Elixir, Lawgiver?" he asked.

"I have no need. I already bear the Mark of the Chosen," responded the leader.

Blade didn't like the implications of that remark. His lips compressed as he contemplated the possibilities. In short order they came to the break in the fence, where someone long ago had snipped the links in a straight line from the bottom to within four inches of the top. Blade waited for the Lawgiver to enter the complex, then he crouched and squeezed through the gap. As he straightened, a movement on the roof of the two-story square building drew his attention, and he saw a man with a rifle watching them.

Aaron and the four guards passed into the facility.

The square building was positioned on the west side of the CHEMITEX plant. To the north, east, and south were the one-story rectangular structures. Above all four reared grimy smokestacks.

The Lawgiver led them to a closed brown door at the rear of the square building. Weeds and brush choked the space between the fence and the building, except for the well-defined footpath. He paused at the door and glanced up, smiling and waving at the man on the roof, who had leaned over the edge to keep an eye on them. "Brother Saul!" he called.

"Lawgiver!" the man responded.

Twisting the knob, the Lawgiver gave the door a shove and stepped inside.

Blade walked over the threshold tentatively, uncertain of

what awaited him. A 35-foot corridor connected to another door. Lining both sides of the hall were dozens of lockers.

"Coming here always stirs fond memories," the Lawgiver commented. "I can remember playing here as a child, and I know every nook and cranny in the plant."

"Do you know a secret passage I can use to escape?" Blade asked.

"There is no escape for the impure. Our Maker's wrath will descend like a specter of death on those who do not have the Mark," the Lawgiver said.

They ambled to the next door.

Blade's eyes widened when he beheld the enormous chamber on the other side. Along the east wall were situated a dozen huge vats. In the middle were benches and cabinets, several crammed with beakers and bottles. A wide mixing tank, filled to the brim with a noxious chemical concoction, occupied the area near the north wall. Pipes projected from the containment walls at both ends. Those on the east were connected to the gigantic vats; those on the west went into the ground.

Three men and two women were seated at a nearby bench. They rose and approached, smiling happily.

"Lawgiver!" a woman exclaimed.

Blade's nostrils registered a pungent odor in the air. He glanced up at the ceiling and spotted a jagged, ten-foot hole in the northwest corner where a portion of the roof had caved in. Dust covered everything.

"How are our converts doing?" the Lawgiver inquired.

"Two have almost converted, but the third is giving us a hard time," answered a skinny man.

"Have you tried increasing his dosage?"

"Yes. But he squirms and locks his mouth shut, and it's next to impossible to get the Elixir down his throat," the skinny man replied.

"I'd like to see the progress they've made," the Lawgiver stated, and looked at the Warrior. "You'll find this extremely interesting."

"I'll bet," Blade muttered.

They walked toward the northwest corner.

The Warrior saw that a chunk of concrete the size of a car had fallen and broken into sizeable bits, and the impact had left a shallow depression in the floor, a miniature crater ten feet in diameter and six inches deep. Into this crater rainwater had dropped through the hole in the ceiling, collecting into a stagnant pool. He also beheld a sight that made him clench his fists and grit his teeth in suppressed rage.

Lying on their backs within a yard of the pool, attired in fatigue pants and nothing else, their arms and legs spread-eagled, were the three missing soldiers from the Civilized Zone, shackled to spikes imbedded in the cement.

"Do you know who they are?" the Lawgiver questioned.

"I know," Blade acknowledged gruffly.

They halted a few feet from the soldiers, two of whom were gazing absently into space. The third looked at the Warrior hopefully.

"These are the ones you were sent to find," the Lawgiver stated. "Notice anything different about them, mercenary?"

Blade did, and he swallowed hard and involuntarily shuddered, his skin crawling as his eyes roved over the bright green splotches covering the two troopers who were staring distractedly. The chest and arms of the third soldier were dotted with faint blemishes.

The Lawgiver snickered maliciously.

"Who are you?" the third soldier abruptly inquired. "I'm Sergeant Whitney. Are you really from the Civilized Zone?"

"I'm Blade," the Warrior said, and he could tell by the manner in which the noncom reacted that Whitney had heard of him.

"Blade! They've caught you too!" Sergeant Whitney exclaimed.

"They think they have."

"I was expecting General Reese to send in a battalion," Whitney said.

"What's wrong with these other two?" Blade asked, nodding at the dazed pair.

"It's the damn Elixir!" Sergeant Whitney responded spitefully. "The bastards have been forcing us to drink it!"

"Not another word out of you, or else!" the Lawgiver barked.

"What can you do that you haven't already done?" Whitney snapped. "Kill me? Go ahead! I'd rather be dead than like you!"

Blade glanced at the pool. Lying next to the edge was a metal dipper. He noticed a moist yellow stain along the eastern rim of the crater, and traced the stain across the floor to one of the pipes jutting from the west end of the mixing tank. The pipe had cracked, allowing the chemicals to seep out. Comprehension dawned, and he looked at the Lawgiver in astonishment.

"Do you understand now, mercenary?"

"I think I do," Blade said. "Did your family use this pool for its drinking water?"

The Lawgiver grinned. "Yes."

"And your father and mother took shelter here a year before you were born?"

"Yes."

Blade stared at the green splotches on the two soldiers, the insight shocking him to his core. The chemicals in the mixing tank had leaked from the cracked pipe and trickled into the pool. "It was the chemicals," he said softly.

The Lawgiver laughed lightly and gestured at the mixing tank. "Yes, again. The chemicals. My parents unwittingly drank from the pool, and the chemicals in the water affected the developing child in my mother's womb—me. They had the same effect on my sister. Embryos, apparently, are extremely sensitive to the presence of certain foreign substances in a mother's system."

"Did your parents develop the splotches?"

"Not fully. They broke out in a green rash periodically, but I suspect they didn't develop the splotches because diluted doses are not very efficacious when administered to mature adults."

"But your children have the marks?"

"Yes. Once introduced into the bloodline, the trait is transmissible from generation to generation."

Blade pointed at the troopers. "And your converts?"

"At full dosage, they take about three days, on average, to break out in spots."

"Full dosage?"

"We administer a dipperful twice a day for three days. That's usually enough."

"But why don't the people you convert resent their conversion? Why don't they turn on you?"

"I can answer that!" Sergeant Whitney interjected. "The damn chemicals do strange things to your mind. You lose your will, your ability to resist, and these bastards brainwash you into believing every word they say!"

"Crude, but essentially accurate," the Lawgiver admitted. "Children born with the marks do not pass through the receptive phase, as I prefer to call the stage where an adult is susceptible to indoctrination. Evidently the chemicals cause an imbalance in adult brains, disorienting them and rendering them ripe for my spiritual edification."

"You mean manipulation," Blade said bitterly.

The Lawgiver shrugged. "I would not expect a crass mercenary to see the light."

"None of this explains how you intend to convert the rest of the human population," Blade commented. "At the rate you're going, it will take you a million years just to convert the Civilized Zone."

A crafty glint radiated from the Lawgiver's eyes. "Not if I introduce the chemicals into the water supply of every town and city."

Blade did a double take. "What?"

"You heard me. All I need to do is capture inhabitants of the Civilized Zone, administer the chemicals and initiate them into the Chosen, then send them back into the Zone to pump the Elixir of Life into selected water tanks and reservoirs," the Lawgiver detailed. "Since the converts from the Civilized

Zone know the Zone so well, they're ideal agents."

"It'll never work," Blade said.

"Oh? Why not?"

"You just said that diluted doses aren't effective. You'd have to add massive amounts to any water supply to convert the residents of a town or city."

"True. We've experimented and performed precise calculations on the amount of chemicals we must add to varying quantities of water."

Blade snorted derisively. "What are your agents going to do? Carry the chemicals in the dipper?"

"Follow me," the Lawgiver directed, and walked toward a door in the north wall.

"Hang in there," Blade said to Sergeant Whitney, and followed the leader of the Chosen. He glanced at the immense mixing tank. The very thought of someone deliberately adding toxic chemicals to a water supply chilled him. He'd known the Lawgiver was a madman, but he'd had no idea exactly *how* insane the man actually was. And he'd been wrong earlier. The Chosen were zombies in a sense—breathing, walking, talking, programmed crazies who had lost all conception of truth, reality, and right and wrong.

The Lawgiver exited the square building and went to the rectangular structure on the north.

Blade glanced absently at the fields beyond the fence to the east, and he observed a herd of wild cattle grazing. The observation did not, at that moment, seem very important.

"Take a look in here," the Lawgiver directed, opening a door and stepping aside. Aaron and two guards joined him.

Blade moved to the doorway, and his mouth dropped open when he laid his eyes on the eight vehicles aligned in a row and facing an enormous metal corrugated door in the east wall. "Tanker trucks!" he blurted out.

"Tanker trucks," the Lawgiver confirmed, beaming. "Eight here, six in another of the buildings. One tank can transport more than enough to convert the residents of an average town."

"You'll never get them into the Civilized Zone," Blade said, although his tone lacked conviction. "They'll stop you at the sentry posts."

"Please. Don't insult my intelligence. We both know the sentry posts are on the major highways. The Civilized Zone Army can't possibly cover every secondary road entering their borders. One of my trucks can slip in under cover of darkness, travel to its destination using only the back roads, deposit its load of chemicals in a reservoir, and return without anyone in authority being any the wiser. Clever, no?"

Blade turned from the doorway, his mind reeling, stunned by the practicality of the plan. The scheme might, just might, succeed.

"Can you imagine what would happen if I sent in fourteen loads at once, all to different towns? Within a week the entire countryside would be in a turmoil as more and more people developed the marks. Pandemonium would reign. The military would be unable to contain the hysteria. Those who break out with the splotches will be confused, scared, feeling like outcasts, desperate for guidance and aid which, of course, I will gladly supply," the Lawgiver said gleefully.

"It won't work," Blade reiterated.

"Give me a valid reason why it won't."

"You're a lunatic."

The Lawgiver cackled, then uttered a surprising, remarkably wise statement. "Since when has sanity ever been a prerequisite to wielding power?"

Blade didn't know what to say. He glanced at the tanker trucks, his features downcast.

"Thank you," the Lawgiver said.

"For what?"

"For your reaction. Why do you think I brought you here? I wanted to test your reaction to my plan, to see if you, an outsider, would acknowledge the viability of my grand design," the Lawgiver said, and paused. "Your expression says it all."

"So what now? Will you try to convert me?"

"Now we shall return to the Temple. And, as I promised, you will shortly meet your Destiny."

Aaron and the two guards laughed.

CHAPTER NINETEEN

"I can't leave you clowns alone for a minute."

"What's that supposed to mean?"

"You cow chips need someone to hold your hands and watch over you every second. I'm gone for a spell, and the Big Guy gets himself captured and you goof off."

"I haven't been goofing off," Geronimo said indignantly.

"Have you tangled with any humongous cockroaches?"

"No."

"Did you bump into any jumbo spiders?"

"No, but—"

"I bet you didn't even stomp any Stompers. Why is it I always do all the work on these runs?"

"You'd better be careful," Geronimo stated.

"Why?"

"At the rate you're going, your nose will be ten inches longer by nightfall."

"Why are you pickin' on my nose?"

"I wouldn't pick your nose with a ten-foot pole."

"Excuse me," said a voice behind them.

The Warriors stopped and turned.

"Do the two of you do this all the time?" Marlon inquired.

"Do what?" Hickok asked.

"Argue," Marlon said.

"We never argue," Geronimo responded. "We engage in enlightened discussion."

"We do?" Hickok said.

"Yep. You babble, and I enlighten you on your mistakes," Geronimo said.

Marlon chuckled and looked at the gunman. "I want to thank you again."

"It was a piece of cake."

"Melanie might be dead right now if not for you," Marlon said. "She told me how you saved her."

"She saved my hide too, so I reckon we're even," Hickok mentioned.

"Not quite. Anything I can do for you, I will," Marlon pledged.

"How much longer until we're there?" Geronimo inquired.

"Kiest Park? About ten, maybe fifteen minutes. I hope the Stompers are still hanging out there. They were last we knew," Marlon mentioned.

"Ten minutes, huh? Then let's vamoose," Hickok suggested. He stared at the line of Chains strung out to their rear.

"Head out!" Marlon declared.

They trekked to the southwest, using the side streets and alleys, ever alert for Stompers or the Chosen.

"That army dude was really ticked off at you guys," Marlon commented idly as they crossed Hampton road.

"Garber *was* a mite flustered at being left behind," Hickok agreed.

"We didn't have any choice," Geronimo said. "At least one of our team has to survive to get word to General Reese. Garber may not like staying with Melanie and those three guards, but he knew we were right. If we don't come back, he'll be able to tell the general everything we've learned so far."

"Which isn't all that much," Hickok noted.

"We know about the Chains and the Stompers," Geronimo stated.

"But we know diddly about the blamed Chosen."

"We know they have Blade, and that's enough."

Marlon glanced at Geronimo. "I should thank you again as well for tending to the spider bites."

"You'll need to watch Melanie closely for a week or so," Geronimo advised. "She lost a lot of blood, which is the reason she fainted, but I don't believe the spiders were poisonous. There was no discoloration or puffiness where she was bitten."

"You think she'll be all right?" Marlon inquired anxiously.

"I know she will," Geronimo said. "In a month she'll be as good as new."

"I was so afraid I was going to lose her," Marlon remarked.

"I know how you feel," Hickok said.

"Have you ever lost a woman you loved?"

"Once," Hickok replied, thinking of the Warrior named Joan, the woman he had loved years ago, before he met his wife. Joan had been slain by the vicious Trolls in Fox, Minnesota. Whenever he thought of her fate, he appreciated having Sherry all the more.

They continued warily, halting briefly five minutes later when a two-headed cat as big as a calf bounded across the road and vanished into a brownstone. They passed the building with their weapons ready, but the feline didn't attack. Seven minutes later a tract of dense vegetation appeared ahead.

"Kiest Park," Marlon announced, and held up his right hand so the column would stop. "What's the next move?"

"Hickok and I will go into the park and look for the Stompers," Geronimo proposed.

"And what if they decide to shoot first and ask questions later?"

"Leave it to me," Hickok said. He slung the Henry over his left shoulder, hooked his thumbs in his gunbelt, and strolled forward.

"Wait for me," Geronimo declared.

"You're both nuts!" Marlon stated, watching them advance. He frowned, looked at the Chains, then scanned the park. "Damn idiots!" he muttered.

"They'll get their fool heads blown off," commented the third man in the line.

"Who asked you?" Marlon snapped, and hitched at his pants.

"What are you mad at me for?" asked the bewildered man.

"I'm not," Marlon said brusquely, and sighed. "I want all of you to stay put."

"Where are you going?" the man queried.

"Where the hell do you think?" Marlon retorted, and ran to catch up to the gunfighter and the Indian. "Wait for me."

Geronimo glanced over his right shoulder as Marlon reached them. "We have company."

"Reeves knows me. We've yelled insults at each other a few times," Marlon said. "He probably won't open fire if he sees me with you."

"We hope," Geronimo responded. He slanted the Browning barrel at the ground and scrutinized the weeds, thickets, and trees. The Stompers had selected an excellent hideaway; no one could approach the park without being seen.

"Let me do the talking," Marlon recommended.

"Fine by me," Hickok said. "I just hope this Reeves hombre has some horse sense. We can't afford to waste time."

Geronimo saw a bush quiver although the air was perfectly still. "They're watching us."

"Then let's get this show on the road," Hickok said, and halted. "We're lookin' for the Stompers!" he called out.

Marlon stepped in front of the gunman. "You said I could do the talking."

"Sorry. By my guest. My lips are sealed."

"That'll be the day," Geronimo cracked.

"Here goes nothing," Marlon said, facing the vegetation 15 yards off and squaring his shoulders. "Reeves! Reeves! You know who this is! I've come here to talk!"

No one responded.

"They might be out scrounging for food," Marlon commented.

"Try again," Geronimo prompted.

"Reeves! This is Marlon! We came here in peace to talk! Can you hear me?"

A tall, brown-haired woman wearing jeans and a leather jacket stepped into view next to a tree. "How do we know this isn't a trick?" she demanded, gazing past the trio at the Chains 50 feet away.

"Who are you?" Hickok asked.

"Cathy."

"Where's Reeves?" the gunman queried.

"He's here."

"Then why doesn't he show himself? Is he a wimp or a man?" Hickok asked caustically.

Marlon leaned close to the gunfighter. "*I'm* supposed to be doing the talking! If you get Reeves mad, we'll never pull this off!"

"I won't say another word," Hickok said.

"Where have we heard that before?" Geronimo quipped.

Two men emerged from the undergrowth accompanied by Cathy. The first stood well over six and a half feet in height and weighed in the vicinity of 250 pounds. Matted shoulder-length black hair hung from his head. His eyes were beady and brown. A dirty, torn gray shirt and overalls bulged at the waist, suggesting budding corpulence. He held a double-barreled shotgun in his pudgy hands.

By contrast, the second man seemed to be all skin and bones. His blue shirt and jeans clung loosely to his thin frame. A shock of blond hair crowned his brow. Clasped firmly and tucked against his right side was an Uzi.

The woman called Cathy had a semiautomatic pistol, resting in a flapped holster on her right hip.

"I'm Reeves!" the large man declared. "Who claims I'm a wimp?" He came within six yards of the trio and halted.

"No one said you're a wimp," Marlon answered quickly.

"Bull! I heard this jerk call me a wimp!" Reeves growled, and wagged his left thumb at the gunman.

"Simmer down, manure-mind," Hickok said calmly. "We wanted to get you out in the open, that's all."

Reeves glanced at the Chains, then at Marlon. "Why? What kind of game are you playing? I'm warning you. One word from me and the Stompers will blow you away."

"This isn't a game. It isn't a trick," Marlon said. "We're here on serious business. I want to offer you a truce so we can join forces against the Chosen."

The head of the Stompers blinked rapidly, his mouth slackening in amazement. "Say *what*?"

"You know as well as I do that the only way we can beat the Chosen is if we combine our gangs," Marlon stated. "We're planning to take them on, and we need your help."

"You've never asked for our help before," Reeves noted suspiciously. "Why now?"

"The Chosen have captured a friend of ours," Geronimo interjected. "We intend to rescue him."

"And who the hell are you?" Reeves snapped. "I've never laid eyes on you or the chump in the buckskins."

"We're from the Family," Geronimo answered.

"The what?"

"The Family is an ally of the Civilized Zone."

"So? Who cares? Your friend means nothing to us," Reeves said.

"They can help us if we'll help them," Marlon declared.

"How can these turkeys help us?" Reeves queried.

"We can assist you in relocating to the Civilized Zone if you'll aid us in freeing our friend," Geronimo mentioned.

The thin man with the Uzi took a half step forward. "Relocate? You'd help us get out of Dallas?"

"That's right," Geronimo assured him.

"What's the Civilized Zone like?" Cathy asked.

"Compared to Dallas, it's paradise," Geronimo told her.

Reeves snorted. "How do you know we can trust these pricks? They could be feeding us a pack of lies."

"I trust them," Marlon said.

"Oh, now *that's* encouraging! As if we'd believe you," Reeves responded, and laughed.

Marlon's features reddened. "Listen, Reeves. You know

that I hate you as much as you hate me. I wouldn't be making this offer if it wasn't genuine. The last thing in the world I'd ever want to do is ask you for help. I know what you're like.''

"Then you know you're wasting your breath," Reeves said.

"Maybe we should listen to them," the thin man ventured.

"No way, Dan," Reeves stated emphatically.

"But if they're serious, this is our chance to get out of this hellhole," Dan commented.

"No."

"What about those of us who have kids?" Dan asked the hulking leader.

"Your kids will be fine. We'll look after them like we always have," Reeves replied.

"But there are fewer and fewer of us every month," Cathy said, chiming in.

"Now don't *you* start!" Reeves said. He glared at Marlon. "You came all this way for nothing, sucker! Don't get lost on your way back."

"I think we should agree to help them," Dan declared stubbornly.

"Tough. You're not the head of the Stompers. I am," Reeves stated arrogantly. "As long as I'm the top dog, what I say goes." He started to turn.

"Hold the fort there, ugly," Hickok suddenly spoke up.

"What the hell do you want?" Reeves snarled.

Hickok looked at the thin man. "If you were in charge of the Stompers, you'd help us?"

"That's right," Dan responded.

What transpired next happened so swiftly that those who witnessed it were shocked speechless by the brutal abruptness of the act. The gunfighter's right hand blurred as the right Python swung up and out, and with the booming of the Colt a hole materialized between Reeves's eyes and the rear of his cranium erupted in a spray of blood and brains. He fell straight backwards, like a mighty oak toppling over in the forest, and thudded on the ground.

The gunfighter twirled the Python into its holster and smiled at the Stomper named Dan. "Congratulations. You're now in charge."

Dan gawked at the blood oozing from the hole in Reeves's forehead. "You shot him!" he blurted out.

Stompers converged on them from the park.

Hickok walked over to the thin man. "You'd best snap out of it. The next move is up to you." His voice lowered menacingly. "And you'd better make the right move, and pronto, or I'm liable to lose my temper."

Dan glanced at the gunman, at those hands hovering near the pearl-handled Colts, and gulped.

CHAPTER TWENTY

Blade stood at the west end of the field, near the uprights, his arms at his sides, staring at the 100 or so members of the Chosen gathered in the stands in front of him to witness whatever had been planned. He recalled the uneventful ride from CHEMITEX back to the stadium, and he wished he had made a break then instead of waiting for a better opportunity to arise. None had, and now, with the sun sinking toward the western horizon but still visible above the stadium wall, he braced himself for the worst. From the wicked grins the Chosen were casting in his direction, he knew the Lawgiver had something diabolical in store for him.

For over an hour the elderly maniac had addressed his followers, exhorting them to stand firm in their commitment to remove the impure heathen from the face of the earth. The Lawgiver had extolled the Chosen as God's special people, a people with a divine mission to perform. He'd quoted from Scripture to justify his statements. The longer he'd talked, the more fanatical he'd become, his arms gesturing animatedly as he inspired them to attain new heights of devotion to the will of the Maker. Again and again he'd stressed his personal relationship with the Maker, claiming that all he did, his every action and thought, was directed by God. And the Chosen had responded to the Lawgiver's pronouncements enthusiastically cheering and applauding after almost every sentence. They were his puppets, and he was the puppet master.

Standing in the lowest row, the Lawgiver now gazed at the Warrior and smiled. "Well, mercenary, the moment of your meeting with Destiny has arrived."

Blade said nothing. He refused to give the Lawgiver any satisfaction by reacting.

"You must be curious about the Destiny I refer to," the Lawgiver said. "I will explain, but first I must offer my gratitude for your kind gifts."

The Warrior's eyes narrowed.

"In all my years I haven't seen a pair of knives in such outstanding condition," the Lawgiver remarked, and leaned down to retrieve the Bowies from the floor near his feet. He held the knives aloft. "Your machine gun will be used to protect our tanker trucks when they enter the Civilized Zone. But I have decided to keep these for myself. Thank you."

Blade's lips compressed tightly.

The Lawgiver lowered the knives. "And now for our evening's entertainment. Perhaps you noticed the wild cattle feeding in the vicinity of our chemical plant?"

Blade wasn't about to admit he had observed the cattle.

"Ranches were once widespread across Texas," the Lawgiver went on. "The Texans prided themselves on their hardy stock, particularly their cattle. After the war, probably millions of head reverted to a wild state. There are many herds in close proximity to Dallas, and they provide us with meat for our table." He paused. "The herd near the plant included a magnificent specimen of longhorn. Are you familiar with the breed?"

As before, the Warrior maintained his silence.

"I had thoughts of domesticating some of them, so I ordered the longhorn to be taken. I envisioned him as the first in the huge herd we would own, but the brute proved to be too wild and intractable. We managed to rope him, but he killed one of my men in the process. I was about to have the animal slain when a wonderful idea occurred to me, no doubt induced by the Maker.''

Blade heard a muted clattering emanating from a tunnel under the stands to his left.

''Occasionally our attempts to convert the impure are not successful,'' the Lawgiver continued. ''Originally, we disposed of them as humanely as they deserved, either by hanging or strangling. But when I saw the longhorn kill poor Brother Elisha, I recognized I was beholding a lethal instrument of the Maker, an ideal killing machine, as it were.''

The clattering had grown in volume until the pounding of hooves on cement was audible.

''So now, when I deem someone as unworthy of belonging to the Chosen, we need not bother with a messy hanging. We simply position them out there, where you are, and unleash their Destiny,'' the Lawgiver said, and smirked. ''Destiny, by the way, is the name we've given our longhorn.''

A moment later the steer burst from the tunnel to the loud cheers of the Chosen.

Blade crouched and tensed, astounded by the beast.

Destiny stood seven feet tall at the shoulders. Rawboned and rangy, the animal had a tough, thick hide brownish red in color. The head was long, the nose blunt and black. Massive muscles rippled and flowed as it moved, and the creature radiated a feral, fierce air, a ferocity accented by the pair of sweeping horns jutting from either side of its head. Monstrous horns they were, with a five-foot spread and curved forward from the center, capable of spearing through a human body with ease.

Blade glanced longingly at the Bowies in the Lawgiver's right hand.

Snorting noisily, Destiny halted and swung its head from side to side. The steer spied the Warrior and began stamping its front hooves on the ground.

How in the world was he going to fight something that size? Blade asked himself, and before he could formulate a strategy the inevitable occurred.

Destiny charged.

Blade focused on the longhorn's head, gauging the distance, barely listening to the pounding of the hooves and the cries of the crowd. He saw the animal lower its head when it was still ten feet off, and he waited until the very last instant to hurl himself to the right as far as he could. He came down on his right side and rolled to his feet in a fluid motion.

The steer had passed him by and wheeled, and was already attacking anew.

"Death to the impure!" someone in the stands shouted.

Blade shut all distractions from his mind. He could see the pointed tips of the longhorn's horns sweeping toward him, and he leaped to the right, his arms outstretched. A hard object gouged into his left calf, causing him to flinch, and he came down hard on his stomach. He rose to his knees and glanced at his calf. A horn had snagged the fabric and his fatigue pants, tearing a hole and puncturing his skin. The wound did not appear to be deep or serious, and he rose quickly and rotated.

Destiny had stopped about 20 feet off and was staring at the Warrior, its nostrils flaring.

Sooner or later the longhorn would get the range. Blade knew he couldn't stay in the open, exposed. But where else could he go? If he tried to run for the stands, the Chosen would open fire. And there was nowhere else on the—

Wait a minute!

The uprights!

Blade looked at the orange posts. They were smooth as glass, but they were the only hope he had. With the realization came action, and he sprinted for the uprights at top speed.

Destiny charged once more.

The earth underfoot seemed to shake as the longhorn bore down. Blade pumped his legs and arms, covering the distance in a rush. He vaulted upward at the nearest vertical post, wrapping his herculean arms around the upright and clinging for dear life.

A tremendous blow struck the post just below the Warrior's dangling legs.

Blade clamped his ankles on the upright and glanced down.

The steer had struck the post, then backed off to shake its head and bellow. He climbed higher, retaining his grip with the greatest difficulty but determined to reach the horizontal crossbar. As he came within 12 inches of the bar, he lunged with his right hand.

Just as Destiny rammed the upright again.

The vibration proved too much for Blade's sweaty arms to resist. He began sliding down, toward the steer's waiting horns, and he frantically strived to check his descent. A cold wind seemed to strike his spine as he gained momentum, and he executed a desperate gambit to save his life. Rather than fall onto those horns and be impaled, he abruptly pushed away from the upright, his arms uncoiling like steel springs, and tried to fling his body to the left, away from the longhorn.

Instead, he slipped.

Blade plummeted, anticipating the burning sensation of having a horn lance through his chest or abdomen. But he missed the steer's head and crashed onto its broad back.

Startled by the unexpected impact and weight, Destiny darted away.

The Warrior tumbled from the longhorn onto his back, the breath whooshing out of him. He scrambled erect, intending to race for the stands despite the consequences, but he was too late.

Destiny had turned sharply and was already on him.

Blade saw the horns arcing at his torso and instinctively reached out, his hands closing on the middle of the horns when the tips were mere inches from him. He endeavored to brace his legs and hold fast, but even though the steer wasn't moving fast the jolt drove Blade backwards a yard. Gritting his teeth, every sinew straining to the limit, he dug in his heels and held on.

The longhorn snorted and tried to wrench loose.

The muscles on Blade's arms and shoulders bulged in stark relief as he applied every iota of his prodigious strength to the task of restraining the steer. Sweat beaded his brow and poured down his sides. A crimson hue tinged his face, and his veins expanded. He recognized it was only a matter of time before Destiny broke free. What then? If he—

Unexpected bedlam broke out in the stands to his rear.

Blade's forehead creased in consternation. He could hear gunfire and screaming and yelling, a veritable din, as if a war was being fought. But who would have the temerity to assault the Chosen in their own Temple? Hickok might, but not even the gunman would take on such overwhelming numbers by his lonesome. Then again, the gunfighter was unpredictable. From the uproar, he gathered the attacking force must be large, and he resisted the temptation to risk a glance over his shoulder. All of his concentration must be applied to holding those deadly horns.

Their silent, titanic struggle continued for over a minute while the clamour in the stands grew.

Stray rounds smacked into the nearby ground.

Blade felt his arms beginning to tire, and he decided to make a move before he became completely exhausted. He took a deep breath, then released the horns and hurtled to the right, twisting his body so he spun toward the longhorn, prepared to meet another charge.

Only Destiny wasn't moving. The steer was staring at the stands, either confused or fascinated by the chaos.

And chaos it was. Blade looked to his left, astounded at the sight of scores of bodies sprawled in the bleachers in attitudes of death. Three fourths of the Chosen had been slain, mowed down in their seats by the surprise attack. Those still able were conducting a running battle with dozens of men and women, and at the forefront of the attacking force were Hickok and Geronimo. Blade saw the gunfighter, a Python in either hand, cut loose at a group of the Chosen poised on a lower tier, and six of the fanatics died in a hail of lead. Somehow, Blade deduced, Hickok and Geronimo and those with them had managed to get above and behind the Chosen.

The Lawgiver's flock never stood a chance.

A solitary figure leaped from the lowest row to the earth, his gaze on the battle to his rear, and raced toward the field.

Blade straightened. It was the Lawgiver! And he still held the Bowies! The Warrior took a stride, planning to cut the Lawgiver off, but his horned adversary was swifter.

Destiny lowered his head and pounded forward.

The Lawgiver didn't realize his danger until the longhorn was less than four feet away. His shocked countenance swung around, and he mouthed the word "No!" And then Destiny's right horn ripped into his chest, tearing through from front to back, and he was lifted from his feet and tossed over the steer's back.

Blade saw his Bowies fly from the Lawgiver's limp fingers, and he ran to reclaim his knives. He saw the Lawgiver crash to the ground, and in seconds the longhorn loomed above the man responsible for its capture, slashing repeatedly with its horns as if it was exacting revenge for its torment. Blade turned his attention from the horrid goring to his knives. In six bounds he reached them, and he scooped the Bowies into his hands with a feeling of relief. Grinning, he pivoted and glanced at the stands.

Most of the Chosen were dead, dying, or had fled.

Hickok and Geronimo were hurrying down an aisle. The gunman looked at Blade, stopped abruptly, and started shouting and motioning with his arms.

What was he—!

Blade whirled, knowing what he would see: Destiny, coming at him with all the raw power of a tank, its horns dripping blood.

This time he was ready.

Blade's right arm swept back, his hand grasping the Bowie by the hilt, timing the throw precisely. The longhorn was 12 feet from him when he whipped his arm down and let go, and the gleaming knife streaked like a razor-edged missile into the steer's left eye, slicing the orb and penetrating deep into the socket. He darted to the right and Destiny thundered by him.

An enraged bellow rent the air as the longhorn slowed, shaking its head, crimson spraying from its ruptured eye.

Shifting the Bowie in his left hand to his right, Blade sprang forward and leaped in close, stabbing the knife into Destiny's neck.

The steer tottered, then recovered some of its strength and lashed out, its left horn lancing at the Warrior.

Blade caught the horn in his left hand, moved in next to the longhorn's neck, and extended his right arm to stab the beast in the other eye. The Bowie sank in nearly to the hilt.

Destiny stiffened, then reared, kicking and pitching.

The steer's neck struck Blade in the chest, and the Warrior was knocked for a loop. He thudded onto his back and lay there, dazed, until his senses suddenly cleared and he could prop himself on his elbows.

Destiny had expired. The longhorn lay on its right side, the hilts of the Bowies sticking from its eyes, a pool of blood forming about its head.

Footsteps pounded close at hand.

"Pard! Pard! Are you all right?"

Blade rose, feeling sore all over, and faced the west end of the stadium.

Hickok and Geronimo ran to his side.

"Are you all right?" the gunman repeated.

"Never felt better," Blade replied.

"We've got those pesky varmints on the run," Hickok declared. "All that's left is the mopping up."

"And we have to rescue the soldiers from the sentry posts," Blade said. He wiped the sweat from his forehead.

"You know where they're at?" Geronimo asked.

Blade nodded. "At a chemical plant General Reese needs to destroy."

"I'm glad to see you're in one piece," Hickok commented. "But then, I reckon I should've known you'd be pulling a Geronimo."

"A what?" Blade said.

"I should've known you'd be goofin' off."

Blade nodded at the dead longhorn. "You call this goofing

off?''

"Sure," the gunfighter said. "What else would you call what you were doing? I saw the whole thing from up on the stands. While we were fightin' for our lives tryin' to wipe out the Chosen, you were down here dancin' with a blamed cow.''

CHAPTER TWENTY-ONE

He answered the knock on the cabin door, wondering who would be paying them a visit at such a late hour. His wizened features creased into a smile when the light from the lantern in his left hand illuminated their faces. "Nathan! Geronimo! You've returned safely."

"Yep," Hickok responded. "Sorry to be bothering you when it's almost midnight, old-timer, but we figured you'd want us to report right away."

Plato stared into the darkness. "Where's Blade?"

"He's fine," Geronimo said. "He's with Jenny and Gabe right this minute."

"And we're headin' home ourselves," Hickok mentioned. "I can't wait to see my missus. She'll be tickled pink that I'm back. Whenever we return from one of these runs, she can't get enough of my pucker power."

Geronimo glanced at the gunman. "Pucker power?"

"Never mind that," Plato said impatiently. "How did Blade fare on the mission?"

"He acted as normal as me," Hickok said.

"He did?" Plato declared, sounding worried.

"Yep. Except for dancin' with a cow, he would've done Jim Bowie proud," Hickok asserted.

Plato looked at Geronimo. "Can you translate?"

"Blade handled the mission efficiently. You have no reason to be concerned."

"What about the plague?"

"There wasn't one," Geronimo answered.

"Yeah. It was just a bunch of yahoos who looked like walkin' asparagus going around drinkin' toxic chemicals and being unsociable," Hickok elaborated.

"I see. I think," Plato said. "Well, I don't want to detain you. I know you're eager to see your families."

"See you in the morning," Geronimo responded.

"Don't let the bedbugs bite," Hickok quipped.

Plato smiled as he closed the door. He paused, listening to their conversation as they moved off.

"Do you mind if I ask you a question?"

"You can ask me anything, pard. You know that."

"What exactly *is* pucker power?"